Loving Him In Pieces

An Of Wolves & Butterflies Novella

by **Brandon Thomason**

For Marilyn, who knew his first laughter,
and Rose, who held his last tenderness.
Your love shaped the boy,
your strength shaped the man,
and your stories deserved to be told.

Important Note to Readers

Before you begin, know this:
This is **not** Gabriel's story.
This is the story of the two girls who loved him, stood by him, hurt because of him, and still carried pieces of him long after their paths separated.
Marilyn and Rose are not side characters here.
They are the heart.
This novella follows the canon of *Of Wolves & Butterflies* closely.
Scenes you recognize remain untouched; nothing is rewritten or contradicted.
Instead, you're invited into the moments we never saw—the childhood memories, the private fears, the quiet acts of loyalty, and the truths they held behind the scenes.
Some chapters deal with themes of trauma, broken trust, emotional fallout, and the weight of loving someone who is unraveling.
Approach with gentleness—for yourself and for them.
If the novel showed Gabriel's descent,
this novella shows the **light** that surrounded him,
and the **cost** of being that light.
I hope their stories stay with you.

"This is not his story.
This is the story of the ones who tried to love him
before he knew how to love himself."

CHAPTER 1
MARILYN

The Boy Everyone Called Good

Before everything got strange, before junior high and different schools and long silences on the phone, Gabriel was just the boy who sat next to me at the blue table in kindergarten and offered me the red crayon without being asked.

He was small for his age, all elbows and big eyes and a cowlick that refused to cooperate. The teachers liked him right away. So did I. He never laughed when I stumbled over words during reading. He would whisper the hard ones under his breath, like a secret we were both in on. When kids picked teams in P.E. and my name came last, he always scooted over so there was room next to him.

It did not take long for people to start saying it.

"He's such a good boy," the teacher would sigh at conferences. "He's such a good boy," the lady at church would tell his mom. "Such a good boy," our neighbor would repeat when he helped her carry in her groceries.

I grew up hearing it about him the way other people grow up hearing their last name. I did not think it was heavy. It was just true. He was good, in the plainest way. Polite. Kind. Soft with people.

We weren't official about it, but everyone knew: if you saw me, he was probably close by somewhere. Recess, field trips, winter programs. We did school projects together. We traded snacks. We swapped stickers. When other girls started whispering about boys in third grade, I kept my mouth shut because nothing about Gabriel felt like a crush. He was just… mine. The friend I trusted without thinking.

By fifth grade, we could talk with our eyes.

I could tell when his math paper was confusing him. He could tell when some other girl's comment had bruised my feelings. He'd nudge my arm lightly if I looked close to tears. I'd roll my eyes when he started one of his weird Titanic fact dumps during lunch and then listen to every word anyway.

So when he told me about Tracy, I paid attention.

"She likes Titanic," he said, like it explained everything. "And turtles."

He said her name like it mattered. Like it did not fit in his mouth yet but he wanted it to.

I met her one afternoon on the playground. She was shorter than me, with freckles sprinkled across her nose and bangs that never stayed in place. She laughed loudly, threw her head back, talked with her hands. She liked being looked at. I understood why he was drawn to her. She was the kind of girl everyone noticed.

"Do you think she likes you?" I asked as we walked home that day.

"I don't know," he said, but his smile said he hoped so.

He talked about taking her to see Titanic like it was not a big deal, then repeated every detail of the night to me afterward. How she held his hand. How she leaned on his shoulder during the sad parts. How she kissed him on the cheek on the porch when it was over.

"I felt like I was floating when I went to bed," he admitted, grinning in a way I had never seen before.

I had no idea you could be happy and uneasy for someone at the same time. I was glad he had that moment. I was also scared of what might happen to it.

Tracy's birthday party was our whole world for about a week. He picked out a turtle lamp for her, the kind with a little stained-glass shell. He'd carried the box around my living room like a sacred object.

"You think she'll like it?" he asked for the tenth time. "Yes, she'll like it," I said, because I needed that to be true.

Her house smelled like vanilla candles and pizza rolls. Kids ran everywhere, their socks slipping on the tile. In the living room, older cousins had put on a movie they had no business watching, all shadows and skin and grown-up jokes. Tracy's mom darted in from the kitchen, flustered and shouting to turn it off.

I was setting cups on the counter when I saw Gabriel in the doorway, shoulders tense, eyes fixed on the TV for a second too long. Then he turned and walked straight down the hall, head down. I felt this odd prickle along my arms, like I'd just seen something important and had no idea what it meant.

"Hey!" I called. "Where are you going?"

He didn't answer. The noise swallowed my voice.

Later, when it was time for presents, he stood off to the side, shifting his weight from foot to foot. Tracy ripped through wrapping paper, squealing over some things, tossing others aside. When she opened the turtle lamp, she gave a quick "Oh, that's cute," and set it down without really looking at it.

I looked at him. His face did not give much away, but his shoulders dropped, just a little. I felt something in my chest drop with them.

On Monday, he was at his locker, staring harder than necessary at his books when I walked up.

"How'd it go?" I asked.

"It was fine." He said it in that flat, tired way that told me it was not fine at all.

A few minutes later, he pressed a folded piece of notebook paper into my hand.

"Can you give this to her?" he mumbled. "Between classes. Please."

"You know I won't read it."

"That's why I'm asking you."

Tracy took the note from me in the hallway with that little crooked smile and tucked it into her binder. I walked away before she could open it. I did not want to see her face if it did not light up.

Our house phone was quiet that afternoon. I kept glancing at it during cartoons, half expecting his number to flash on the caller ID. It never did.

The next morning, his eyes looked puffy, like he had either slept badly or cried and didn't want anyone to know.

"She doesn't want to go out anymore," he said when I caught him before homeroom.

"What? Why?" He shrugged. "Doesn't matter. It was stupid anyway."

He tried to laugh. It came out thin. That was the first time I felt like something had reached into his chest and taken a piece, and he was pretending not to notice.

I didn't find out the words she used—*I only went out with you because I felt sorry for you*—until much later. But even without the script, I knew it had been cruel.

That was when the phrase "good boy" started sounding different in my head.

People kept saying it. He started hearing it like a consolation prize.

We finished fifth grade. Summer passed in bike rides and sprinklers and long afternoons, but he was quieter when Tracy's name came up. He still walked me home. Still bumped my shoulder when I got quiet. But there was a sliver of distance that hadn't been there before. I could feel it even when I couldn't see it.

Sixth grade brought Jo.

She wasn't loud like Tracy, just quietly pretty. Straight dark hair, careful eyeliner, the kind of girl who always had gum and knew the right things to say. The first time I noticed her with him was at lunch, when she slid a folded note across the table and his whole posture changed.

He did not gush about her the way he'd done with Tracy. This time it was more guarded, like he did not trust happiness to stick.

"She's nice," he said. "She doesn't think I'm weird for liking orchestras and disasters."

"That's a weird combination," I pointed out.

He laughed, but there was a question behind it, like *Are you sure it's okay that I'm like this?*

"Do you like her?" I asked one day as we walked across the field.

He kicked a rock and watched it skid. "I don't know. Maybe."

But he kept every note she passed him. That told me more than he would.

When he told me he was taking her ice skating, I smiled even though something in me tightened up.

"What if I fall?" he asked.

"Then you fall," I said. "It's ice. That happens."

"She said if she falls, I have to catch her."

He said it soft, like it was something fragile he didn't quite know how to hold.

He came back from the rink glowing, describing the way she clung to his arm, how she pretended to wobble so he'd steady her. It sounded small, but to him it was everything.

Then the letter came.

We were sitting on the curb again, end of the school day, when he pulled it out of his pocket. The paper was already creased from where he'd folded and unfolded it.

"She gave me this after lunch," he said.

"Do you… want me to read it?" I asked.

"No. I'll do it."

He read it in a monotone, like he could keep it from getting under his skin if he drained all feeling out of it. She wrote about going to different schools next year. About thinking he was "really sweet." About hoping he found "a good girl." About him being "a good boy."

There it was. Again.

He exhaled, a sharp breath through his nose, and folded the page in on itself, smaller and smaller, until his fingers couldn't make it any tinier.

"You okay?" I asked.

"I'm fine," he said, staring at the street. "It's not like we were going to get married or anything."

Sixth graders weren't supposed to talk about getting married. He said it like a joke that felt too close to the truth.

After winter break, Jo showed up in the hallway talking to Tye. I hadn't seen Tye in a long time—he dipped in and out, the kind of boy who made teachers anxious and other boys want to follow him. Jo laughed at something he said and touched his arm.

I looked at Gabriel. His face barely moved. If I didn't know him, I would have thought he hadn't noticed. But I knew him. His jaw was too tight.

"You okay?" I whispered.

"Yeah," he lied.

He didn't talk about Jo much after that. Or Tracy. Or any of it, really. It all sank into this quiet, heavy place inside him that he wouldn't let me near.

And then, without anything dramatic happening that I could point at, he just… changed.

Not all at once. Inches at a time.

He started flinching more when someone raised their voice. His laugh came out wrong sometimes, like he was performing it. He'd stop talking in the middle of sentences and say "Never mind." He stared off in class like he was somewhere else. When I asked what he was thinking about, he'd shrug or make a joke.

Sometimes he still felt like the boy from kindergarten. Sometimes he felt like someone older wearing that boy like a costume.

"Are you sure you're okay?" I asked one afternoon as we walked home past the same cracked sidewalk we'd crossed a thousand times.

"I'm fine," he said, but he wouldn't look at me.

I tried to tell myself it was normal. People changed. We were growing up. We were going to different junior highs soon. Maybe this was just what "almost twelve" did to people. Boys got weird. Girls got weirder. Maybe I was imagining it.

But the last day of sixth grade, when we sat on the curb again and watched the bus drive away for the summer, I felt that same twisting in my stomach I'd felt the day he told me about Tracy breaking up with him. Like something had slipped out of place and I didn't know how to put it back.

He bumped my shoulder. "See you this summer?"

"Yeah," I said. "You better call."

"I will."

He smiled, but it didn't reach his eyes all the way.

I didn't know it yet, but that was the end of the uncomplicated version of us. Of him. Of the boy everyone called good like it was a shield powerful enough to protect him from anything.

I would spend years trying to understand why it didn't.

CHAPTER 2
MARILYN

The Year Everything Went Quiet

I thought seventh grade would feel like sixth grade with slightly bigger backpacks. I didn't expect much to change—new teachers, new classrooms, new kids I'd forget the names of by winter. The only real difference was that Gabriel and I would be at different schools. That scared me more than I liked to admit, but I kept telling myself he'd call. He always called.

And for a while, he did.

At first, it was just the usual stuff. We'd both get home, drop our bags, and one of us would call the other on the house phone. His voice sounded a little deeper—thirteen will do that—but the way he filled the silence was the same. He complained about homework. I told him the drama happening in my English class. He told me about a kid in his science class who kept tapping his pencil. I made him laugh about the awful cafeteria pizza.

It felt like us. It felt safe. It felt like nothing would break.

Then one afternoon in late September, he called, and everything was different.

He said "hello," and something in my stomach dropped. His voice wasn't just deeper—it was hollow. Like all the color had drained out of it. Like he was speaking from the other side of something I couldn't see.

"Hey," I said, sitting up straighter on my bed. "What's wrong?"

"Nothing," he replied too quickly.

"You sound weird."

"I'm tired," he said, again too quickly.

I pushed my thumbnail against the spiral of my notebook, trying to understand the wrongness. He sounded not like a bad day wrong—this was deeper. Like something had happened and he was keeping both hands over the wound.

"What happened?" I asked quietly.

"Nothing," he repeated.

But there was a tiny tremble in the word. Not enough for most people to catch. But I caught it.

"What did you do today?"

"School."

"Did you sit with anyone at lunch?"

"Does it matter?"

It wasn't mean. It wasn't even sharp. Just empty. Like someone had scooped the warmth out of him and left a shape that sounded like his voice but didn't feel like him.

I tried again. "Gabriel... did something happen?"

Silence. Not long enough to be dramatic, just long enough to be unsettling.

He inhaled through his nose sharply. "I don't want to talk about it."

"Okay," I said softly. "Then you don't have to. We can talk about something else."

"No," he said. "I… I gotta go."

"But—"

The line clicked.

I sat there holding the phone long enough that the dial tone started its low hum. My room felt too quiet. The world felt off balance.

He had never hung up on me before.

…ƒ…

He didn't call for days after that. Each afternoon I'd walk home, open my backpack, do my homework, and glance at the phone every few minutes like I could will it to ring.

It didn't.

When I finally broke and called him, his mom answered and told me he was in his room and "wasn't coming to the phone right now." She said it gently, but something about her tone made me nervous.

The second time I called, she said he was busy.

With what? He didn't play sports. He didn't do clubs. He didn't have a million friends.

I knew in my chest something had cracked, but I didn't know the shape of it.

When he finally called again, the lightness in his voice was gone. He talked about school like he was reading notes off a cue card. When he laughed, it sounded forced, like he was trying to imitate an old version of himself.

I told myself maybe it was puberty. Maybe boys got weird at thirteen. Maybe he was embarrassed about something.

But the fear in his voice didn't sound like puberty.

It sounded like pain.

…ƒ…

The next time we saw each other in person was at the park. I had ridden my bike there after dinner, hoping we'd run into each other the way we used to. He showed up a few minutes later, hands shoved deep into his pockets, eyes darting away from mine.

I tried to make it normal. "Race you to the swings?"

He didn't even smile. "I'm too old for that."

"You're barely thirteen," I said. "No one's too old for swinging."

He shrugged and kicked at the grass.

I walked toward the swings anyway, sat down, and started rocking gently, waiting for him to follow like he always did.

He didn't. He stood there staring at the ground, jaw tight, shoulders hunched.

"Come on," I said. "It's just a swing."

"I said no!" he snapped.

The sound hit me like a slap. I froze, boots dragging in the dirt until I stopped completely. He looked as shocked as I felt, like he hadn't meant for it to come out that way.

"I'm sorry," he muttered. "I didn't… I'm just tired."

He wasn't tired. Kids get tired. They don't break in half like

14

that over a swing.

I nodded, pretending it didn't hurt. "It's okay. Let's just walk."

We walked the long way home without talking much. Every few steps, he'd inhale like he wanted to say something, but the words never came.

When we reached my street, he mumbled "See you" and turned away before I could answer.

I watched him walk off, that hunched shape of him shrinking down the road. I wanted to run after him. I didn't.

Something told me if I pushed too hard, he'd disappear completely.

…ƒ…

Winter came, cold and sharp.

We talked on the phone less and less. Sometimes he'd return a call. Sometimes he wouldn't. When he did, he sounded far away no matter what volume he spoke at.

One night he called late, long after my sisters were asleep. The moment I heard his voice, I knew something was wrong. He sounded small. The kind of small a thirteen-year-old boy tries desperately not to be.

"You okay?" I whispered into the receiver.

A long, shaky breath. "I don't know."

I sat up straighter. "Do you want to talk about it?"

"No."

"Do you want me to stay on the phone?"

A beat. "Yeah."

So I stayed. Neither of us talked. I could hear him

breathing—uneven, shaky at first, then slower.

After a few minutes, he said, "Marilyn?"

"Yeah?"

"Do you think people can change in one day?"

The question was too big. Too heavy. Too full of something he was afraid to name.

"I think," I said carefully, "sometimes something big can happen in a day. But the change… the change takes time."

Silence.

"Are you scared?" I asked quietly.

A tiny voice: "Yeah."

My throat tightened. "Whatever it is, you can tell me."

"I can't." It came out strangled.

"Okay," I whispered. "Then you don't have to."

We sat in silence again. He hung up without saying goodbye.

I cried into my pillow until I fell asleep.

…f…

Eighth grade didn't fix anything.

He grew taller. His voice settled. His shoulders broadened. But emotionally he felt smaller. Like he was folding into himself inch by inch. We passed each other sometimes—church events, mutual friends, the grocery store—but each time he felt a little further away.

He was polite. He smiled. He asked how I was.

But it was all surface. Nothing underneath.

He never talked about school. Never talked about friends. Never talked about feelings. He just existed in this numb, blank space he pretended was normal.

But I'd known him too long to be fooled.

He was hurting. Badly. And alone.

One night, I held the phone after dialing his number, listening to it ring and ring before his mom said he was "not up for talking tonight."

Not up for talking. At thirteen.

I didn't know what that meant. I didn't know what had happened. I just knew something had stolen parts of him, and I hated it.

…ƒ…

Ninth grade was even worse.

We barely spoke. He avoided calls. When he did pick up, the conversation lasted a minute, maybe two. He didn't laugh. Not the real laugh—the one from the old days. He had a new laugh now, sharp and hollow, like he was going through the motions.

I saw him at the store once, leaning on a shopping cart. He looked over at me and forced a smile that didn't reach his eyes. My whole body ached with the memory of who he used to be.

After that day, I wrote his name in the back of my notebook and stared at it for a long time.

I missed someone who was still alive. Nothing prepares you for that.

He would call sometimes—late, quiet, sounding both guilty and relieved that I answered.

"Hey," he'd say. "Hey," I'd whisper back.

I waited for the day he'd tell me the truth. It never came.

I learned to love him through absence. Through silence.

Through the fear that the boy I grew up with was gone for good.

But I stayed anyway. Because someone had to remember who he had been when he couldn't remember it himself.

CHAPTER 3
ROSE

The Girl of Five Sisters

People always told us our house sounded like a stampede, and honestly, I never argued. With five sisters under one roof, there was never a quiet moment. Someone was always yelling about missing shoes, someone was crying over a hair straightener, someone was blasting music through the bathroom door. I grew up learning to weave myself through all that noise without getting swallowed by it.

I was the third-born — squarely in the middle.

Two older sisters who moved with the confidence of people who always got the bathroom first. A little sister just a year behind me, who copied everything I did. And the youngest, three years down, who clung to all of us with sticky popsicle hands.

Being right in the center meant I learned early how to observe without taking up space, how to hear things before they were said, how to read tension like weather patterns. The middle is where you learn to bend. To mediate. To soften the harder edges of a family that's always pulling in different directions.

And behind all that noise was my mother — worn out, overworked, but holding all of us together with a tired kind of love. She never complained about my father leaving. She never named the ache he left behind. She just kept going, and we followed her lead.

My memories of my father are more like atmospheres than scenes. My older sisters talked about how he used religion like a hammer, quoting scripture the way people quote threats. I didn't remember the sermons — just the discomfort. The tightening in my chest at the idea of a God who was always watching, always judging, always disappointed.

Church didn't feel like home after he left. Music did.

…ƒ…

When I was nine, the school orchestra played in our cafeteria, and it felt like someone opened a door to a world that could finally hold all the emotions I didn't know what to do with. I begged my mom for a cello. She couldn't afford it at first, so I waited. Saved birthday money. Did extra chores. Then one day she came home with a rental case that smelled like dust and old wood.

I practiced until my fingers hurt. My sisters complained endlessly. I didn't care. Music didn't yell at me. It didn't demand anything. It didn't break promises. It just existed, steady and soft, giving shape to everything inside me.

Around the time I turned eleven — early sixth grade — we got a computer in the living room. A bulky beige monitor, dial-up that screeched like it was being murdered, and an internet connection that cut off every time someone picked up the phone.

20

It was magic.

My older sisters used it for instant messaging boys and printing pictures of celebrities. I used it to search for music. Songs that felt like truth. Words that echoed the parts of me I didn't speak out loud.

That's how I found Evanescence before anyone around me knew the name.

I stumbled onto a fan page one night, the dark kind with purple fonts and poorly cropped photos. Someone had uploaded MP3s labeled "demo_2000" and "Imaginary early." I downloaded them on LimeWire, hoping they weren't viruses. When I pressed play on the early version of *"My Immortal,"* the unpolished one, raw and echoing like someone recorded it in a bedroom, something in me split open.

Amy Lee's voice spoke the language of all the emotions I didn't know how to name — the ache, the fear, the wanting, the softness. Evanescence didn't feel dark to me; it felt honest.

That led me down a rabbit hole of music that most kids my age didn't listen to. Nirvana became another secret world I loved. *"Come As You Are"* felt like an invitation I didn't understand but desperately hoped was for me. I found *"All Apologies"* on another sketchy download and memorized the guitar line until it lived under my skin.

My sisters teased me for liking "sad music," but it never felt sad. It felt real. It felt like it belonged somewhere deep in me, somewhere words couldn't quite reach.

…ƒ…

Another escape was books — especially ones with shadows in them.

The first time I picked up an Anne Rice novel from the library, I felt like I'd stolen something forbidden. Her stories were lush and haunting and full of longing I didn't have words for yet. I read them at night with a flashlight, the pages glowing under blankets while the rest of the house roared and hummed around me.

Books made me feel like my quietness wasn't a flaw — it was depth.

Music let me feel big feelings without drowning. Stories let me imagine a world where darkness wasn't always dangerous.

These two things shaped me long before any boy ever tried to.

…ƒ…

Then my oldest sister had her first baby.

I thought becoming an aunt would just be a title, not a transformation. But the moment he was placed in my arms — soft cheeks, tiny fists, warm sleep-heavy breath — I felt something shift inside me. Something warm. Something protective.

When she had another son, it only deepened.

Those boys taught me the kind of love that doesn't ask anything back. They taught me how to be soft without being scared. They taught me that gentleness can be powerful.

I used to sit with them on the couch, coloring books spread out, the TV playing cartoons, and I'd think, *If people were just a little gentler with each other, maybe things wouldn't break so easily.*

Those boys saw the best in everyone. Maybe that's why I started wanting to see the best in people too.

By eighth grade, life felt like a familiar pattern — sisters arguing, cello practice, school, my nephews climbing all over me like I was playground equipment. I wrote stories in a journal I hid under my pillow. I listened to music that felt like emotion turned into electricity. I tiptoed around church, wanting God but afraid of Him at the same time.

I tried so hard to be good. Not perfect. Just good.

Gentle. Understanding. Steady.

And deep in my chest, I kept this tiny hope — not for a fairy tale, not for some dramatic romance, but for someone who saw me. Someone who didn't need me to be louder or sharper or anything but what I already was.

Someone whose softness met mine.

But that dream felt far away.

I didn't know that across town, a boy I'd never met was unraveling and trying to sew himself back together with threads too thin to hold. I didn't know he carried wounds he'd never show me. I didn't know he had a goodness that was being buried under things no one warned him about.

I didn't know his name. I didn't know his story. I didn't know he would one day look at me like I held something he'd lost long ago.

All I knew was my music, my books, my sisters, my nephews, my quiet ache.

And life was about to change, even though I had no idea who Gabriel was or how much he would come to mean to me.

CHAPTER 4
MARILYN

The Good Parts That Still Lived

If I'm honest, there were moments in 10th grade where I convinced myself everything would be okay. Not because anything was actually fixing itself, but because every now and then Gabriel would let slip one of those little flashes of who he used to be. They came without warning — like catching sunlight between storm clouds — and each time, I held onto them harder than I probably should have.

The first time it happened was two weeks into the school year. I was in the courtyard during lunch, sitting on the stone ledge under the oak tree, trying to finish a history worksheet. Gabriel wandered over, tray in hand, looking lost in that quiet, distracted way he had started doing lately. He stopped a few feet away, like he wasn't sure if he was allowed to sit with me.

"You can sit," I told him, nudging the empty space beside me.

He blinked as if surprised, then eased down onto the ledge. His shoulders relaxed, just a touch.

For a few minutes, we didn't talk. I chewed my straw. He peeled the label off his water bottle, tiny pieces fluttering to the ground. And then—out of nowhere—he made a joke about the cafeteria chicken nuggets being made from "discount meteorites." It wasn't a good joke, not really, but he delivered it with this sideways grin that threw me straight back to fifth grade.

I laughed. He smiled — actually smiled — and something in my chest loosened for the first time in months.

"See?" I nudged him. "You're still funny."

"I try," he said, shrugging like it didn't matter, but the way his eyes brightened told me he needed to hear that more than he'd admit.

For the rest of lunch, he felt almost normal. He even stole one of my fries. That might seem small to most people — a stolen fry is barely a blip — but when you're watching someone drift away piece by piece, a stolen fry feels like a miracle.

…ƒ…

A week later, I saw a part of him teachers always loved — the part that helped without asking.

I was heading down the east hallway after fourth period when I noticed a sophomore girl crying by her locker. Books were scattered across the floor. Kids were streaming around her like she wasn't even there. I was just about to walk over when I saw Gabriel already crouched beside her, gathering her notebooks.

26

"It gets better," he said gently, offering the stack with both hands like it was something fragile. "High school's loud at first. You'll figure out how to tune it out."

The girl sniffled, wiping her face with her sleeve. "Thanks."

He nodded, quiet as ever, and walked away before she could say anything else.

He didn't see me watching, and something about that made the moment feel even more real — unperformed, unguarded, just Gabriel being good without needing credit.

I pressed a hand to my chest. The boy I loved — the boy I grew up with — was still in there. Buried, maybe. But not gone.

…ƒ…

But the shadows were creeping in too.

Some days he was bright and warm. Other days he came to school looking like he hadn't slept, eyes puffy, posture slumped. And every once in a while, I'd catch him lingering in certain hallways — waiting for someone.

I didn't know the name then. Didn't know the green-eyed boy hovering around the edges. Didn't know the way Gabriel's stomach probably flipped when he saw him.

All I knew was that Gabriel kept glancing toward the band hall entrance as if expecting someone to step through it. Someone I didn't know. Someone he hadn't told me about.

Once, during passing period, his face lit up — this little spark, soft but unmistakable — and I turned my head just in time to see a pale-skinned boy slipping through a crowd across the hall. Dark hair. Sharp expression. Eyes that flicked to Gabriel for a second too long before disappearing into the flow of students.

27

Gabriel didn't move toward him. Didn't wave. Didn't call out.

He just watched him leave, expression unreadable.

I felt something cold settle in my stomach. Not jealousy. Not yet. Just... unease.

Something was happening to him again, and I didn't know what shape it was taking.

…ƒ…

Still, between those strange moments, Gabriel had days where he genuinely seemed okay.

In orchestra, he sometimes leaned toward me during tuning to whisper sarcastic commentary about our director's "dramatic hand flourishes." Once, during rehearsal, his bow slipped on a shift and made an awful squeak, and he burst into real, breathless laughter. Not the fake laugh he'd been practicing all year — the real one that crinkled the corners of his eyes. Half the class looked over, startled. They hadn't heard that laugh yet.

I treasured it.

Another day, after school, he walked with me to the courtyard before his mom picked him up. The orange light of sunset made him look younger, softer. We talked about nothing — the weather, homework, that teacher who kept saying "irregardless" like it was a real word. Then he stopped walking, shoved his hands in his pockets, and said quietly:

"I'm glad we're at the same school again."

My throat tightened. "Me too."

He nodded once, gaze drifting to the parking lot. "It makes things... easier."

"Easier how?"

He hesitated. Eyes flicked down. "Just... easier."

I didn't push. I wanted to, but I didn't. I had learned the hard way that if you push too hard, he slips further away.

Still, the warmth in his voice stayed with me the whole evening.

...ƒ...

But with the good came the strange.

Sometimes he'd show up to orchestra buzzing — that small, bright spark in his eyes again — but he wouldn't tell me why. Other days he'd snap at me for no reason, then apologize immediately like he couldn't control the words escaping his mouth.

He'd lean close to whisper something funny one day... then avoid me the next. He'd share half his granola bar with me at lunch... then shut down when I asked if something was wrong. He'd walk me to class... then walk past me in the hallway like he didn't see me at all.

It felt like loving someone during a thunderstorm — you never knew which part of the weather you'd get.

And then came the day in orchestra when he froze mid-tuning, eyes locked on the band hall doorway. I followed his stare and saw him again — the pale boy with the dark hair, leaning in the frame like he'd been standing there long enough to memorize Gabriel's breathing.

That moment — just that — was enough to change the air in the room.

Gabriel's face flickered with something that wasn't quite fear and wasn't quite joy. Something electric. Something dangerous.

I didn't know his name then. Didn't know the story yet. Didn't know the ache that tethered them together.

But I knew this: Something was pulling Gabriel again. Something strong. Something that didn't leave room for me.

And I knew — before Autumn burst into the room demanding answers — that I was losing him.

Not because he wanted to leave me. But because something else had found him first.

…ƒ…

We hadn't reached the blow-up yet — the shouting, the accusation, the cross at my throat, the prayer I whispered into the air. That moment was still coming.

But even now, at the edges of the year, I felt the shift.

Good Gabriel flickered in and out like a dying lightbulb. Traumatized Gabriel stood right behind him, waiting to take over. And whatever he saw in the boy at the doorway?

It made the darkness move faster.

I held onto every soft moment, every laugh, every reminder of the boy I'd grown up with — because deep down, I knew I was collecting memories of someone I was about to lose.

30

CHAPTER 5
MARILYN

The Year a Stranger Took His Eyes

By the time we got to tenth grade, I had this quiet little hope running under everything: maybe seeing Gabriel every day again would fix what distance had broken.

Ninth grade had felt like walking around with a bruise no one else could see. He and I lived in different worlds, different schools, different routines. Our calls had shrunk to once-a-week check-ins, then once-in-a-while, then whenever he felt like dialing at eleven p.m. and pretending nothing was wrong. I told myself high school would be different. Same building. Same schedule block. Fewer excuses.

For the first couple of weeks, it almost felt true.

We would pass each other in the hallway and he'd give a small smile, a nod, sometimes a quick "Hey, Mar." It wasn't the old days. It wasn't us at the blue kindergarten table. But it was something. Enough to make me think maybe I'd been overly dramatic about losing him.

Then little things started to change.

He'd show up to orchestra with this far-away look, like he'd left half his thoughts somewhere else. Some days he seemed lighter, almost… lit from the inside. Not happy exactly, but charged. Other days he was gone behind his eyes in a way that made my stomach twist.

He'd linger by the doors a bit too long after class, checking his phone. He never used to be like that. He'd walk into the band hall late, bow case already open like he'd been somewhere else and sprinted to beat the bell. He'd stare at nothing during warmups. When I asked if everything was okay, he'd say, "Yeah, why?" like I was the one imagining things.

I wasn't. I had known him too long to miss when something was pulling at him.

I met Autumn around then too. She was new that year, all sharp lines and sharper honesty. Big hair, big personality, boots that clicked down the hallway like punctuation. While I tended toward soft questions, Autumn preferred straight cuts.

"You're Marilyn, right?" she'd said one day in orchestra, dropping into the empty chair beside me like she'd always sat there. "You and Gabriel go way back."

"Since forever," I'd answered, a little proud and a little sad all at once.

She'd watched him across the room as he tuned his cello, head bent low, jaw tight. "He always look like the world's about to fall on him?"

"Not always," I said. "Just… lately."

Her eyes narrowed like she'd just heard a puzzle she intended to solve.

It got worse slowly. That was the hardest part. There wasn't one moment where everything shattered—more like a million tiny hairline cracks spreading across glass. He'd miss lunch with us and say he'd "got held up." He'd vanish between classes and shrug when I asked where he'd been. Sometimes he'd be lighter than I'd seen him in years, almost giddy, only to snap at the smallest thing the next day.

And he kept looking toward the door.

Like he was waiting for someone.

…*f*…

The day everything boiled over started out ordinary. Gray sky, buzzing fluorescent lights in the band hall, stands clattering as we set up for rehearsal. I watched Gabriel from my chair, the way his fingers fidgeted on the bow, the way he kept glancing toward the doorway like he could feel someone there.

I heard the hallway before I saw anything—voices, footsteps, the usual pre-class chaos. Then the room shifted. It was subtle, like a change in air pressure. Gabriel's shoulders tensed. His eyes flicked to the side.

I followed his gaze.

A boy stood just outside the band hall doorway. Jet-black hair spiked in sharp angles, skin pale, eyes so green they seemed to carry their own light. He wasn't smiling. Wasn't talking. Just… watching. Watching Gabriel like there was no one else in the room.

My heart knocked once against my ribs, hard.

"Who the hell was that?" Autumn's voice snapped from the doorway, slicing through the quiet. She strode in like a storm, arms crossed, eyebrow arched into a weapon. She'd clearly seen him too.

I turned and saw her standing there, blocking the frame, every line of her body sharp with suspicion. I hovered a step behind her, hands folded against my chest. I could feel my own worry like a weight I'd been carrying for weeks.

Gabriel froze, bow still in his hand.

"Well…?" Autumn demanded.

He fumbled. "He's just a guy I met the first day of school when we picked up our schedules. Not a big deal. Honestly, I didn't think I'd ever see him again."

"Just a guy?" Autumn's voice could have cut glass. "Seemed like a pretty big deal with the way he was staring at you. Like some creeper."

I flinched at the word. Creeper. It felt too sharp, thrown too hard. But part of me had seen it too—the intensity, the way the strange boy's gaze had lingered like a hook.

"He was just being polite," Gabriel snapped, louder than I'd heard him in a long time. "He's not from here. Maybe that's how people are where he's from. Just respectful."

My chest squeezed. The word sounded wrong in his mouth. Forced. Defensive. He kept talking, words tumbling out faster than his usual careful pace.

"And he's not a creeper. You don't even know him."

Autumn planted a hand on her hip. "Hard to get to know someone when they're entranced by you."

"He wasn't entranced by me! Don't be ridiculous—and what are you implying, Autumn?" His voice cracked a little on her name, part anger, part… fear.

I wanted to step in, to soften it, to tell her to back off and him to breathe. I parted my lips to speak, then closed them again. The air between them felt like it would shatter at the slightest nudge.

Autumn lifted her hands like surrender flags. "I'm not implying anything. Just don't ignore your friends for some guy you barely know."

He'd been doing that more and more—drifting, vanishing, half-here and half-gone. Every time he looked at his phone and smiled at something unsaid, I felt the distance stretch.

Something inside him snapped.

"I wasn't trying to ignore you," he burst out. "Excuse me for feeling good about myself for once. Excuse me for letting someone talk to me like they actually wanted to know me."

The words landed heavy. Not just at Autumn. At both of us.

My lips parted. I wanted to tell him I had always wanted to know him. That I had spent our whole lives wanting to know him. That I had watched him disappearing for years and still stayed. But I wasn't sure he was capable of hearing any of that right then.

So I did what I always did.

I stayed.

Autumn's face twisted, hurt flashing across it before she covered it with a scoff. She bit her lip, exhaled sharply, and turned on her heel, boots clicking out of the room.

For a second, everything in me screamed to run after her. To go with the person who wasn't currently building a wall between us and calling it self-protection. But I didn't move.

I looked at him instead.

He stood there, jaw clenched, eyes burning with something that wasn't anger exactly, but close. He looked like he wanted to be anywhere but inside his own skin.

Anger rolled in my chest, hot and tight—not at him, but at whatever was doing this to him. Whatever had taken the boy I grew up with and twisted him into someone who looked at love like it was a threat.

My hand moved before my brain caught up.

I slipped my fingers into his.

His palm was cold, clammy almost, like he'd been holding tension for hours. I squeezed gently, grounding him, grounding myself. With my other hand, I reached up and touched his cheek, my thumb trembling against his skin.

"Gabriel…" I whispered, searching his eyes for the boy I knew was still in there somewhere. "This isn't you. I'm worried about you."

For a heartbeat, I saw it—the softness, the uncertainty, the old Gabriel peeking through the cracks. His eyes glistened, just a little, like some part of him wanted to collapse into the space I was offering.

Stay here, I wanted to say. Stay where people love you. Stay where you're known.

Instead, he broke eye contact.

He turned his face away and gently slipped his hand from mine. The loss of his fingers in my palm felt colder than the air-conditioning ever could. I watched him retreat into himself in real time.

He walked past me to his chair without another word.

I stood there, my hand still hovering in the space where his had been. Automatically, my fingers went to the little cross at my throat. I curled around it like it was some kind of anchor and whispered a prayer I wasn't sure how to finish.

Help him. Help me not give up on him. Please.

He lowered his bow to the cello strings and started to play. From a distance, it sounded like any other rehearsal—notes, rhythms, a low hum of music filling the room. But I saw his shoulders tight, his jaw tense, his gaze fixed somewhere far away.

He wasn't with us. He was wherever that boy with the green eyes was. Wherever that new attention lived.

I took my seat in the flute section, heart heavy, hands still shaking. Autumn shot me a look from across the ensemble—hurt, guarded, arms crossed like armor. Gabriel sat between us in the orchestra, physically close but emotionally miles away.

For the first time, I realized the terrifying truth:

There were places in him I would never reach. There were rooms inside his heart I did not have the key to. And now there was someone else standing in the doorway, holding his gaze like it belonged to him.

I still loved him. I still remembered who he'd been.

But as I watched him play that day, eyes far off, shoulders tight, I understood:

I wasn't just losing the boy I grew up with. I was losing him to a stranger whose name I didn't even know yet.

And there was nothing I could do but watch and pray and hope that somewhere under all that ache, the real Gabriel was still there.

Waiting to be found.

Maybe not by me. But by someone.

CHAPTER 6
ROSE

First Light

Orchestra days always started the same for me: lugging my cello through the hallway like a clumsy sidekick, weaving between clusters of people who seemed to be in ten different conversations at once. I never fit into the noisy flow of the school, but the orchestra room? That place had always felt like a kind of sanctuary — warm lights, the soft buzz of tuning strings, sheet music scattered across stands like a secret language we all knew.

That morning, everything felt normal.

Until it didn't.

I walked into the room, adjusting the strap on my cello case, and I noticed someone sitting in the far corner of the cello section. A boy I didn't recognize. He had his case open at his feet and was tightening the bow hair with quiet, deliberate movements, like he'd done it a thousand times but didn't want anyone to notice.

He kept his shoulders slightly hunched, as if bracing

himself from something. Not from the room — from himself.

He glanced up the second I saw him.

It wasn't a long look. Not dramatic. Not cinematic.

But something in his eyes made the air between us shift — just a fraction — like a bow pulled lightly across a string.

He looked away quickly, and I forced myself to move, to sit, to pretend that nothing had happened.

I took my seat two chairs down from him. Close enough to see him clearly. Far enough that I didn't look like I had chosen the spot intentionally.

I set my cello upright and let my fingers brush the strings, grounding myself. Then I stole a glance at him.

He was handsome — not in the loud, confident way boys at this school tried to be, but in a quiet way. A tired way. His hair fell slightly past his eyebrows, messy but soft. His eyes were dark and deep-set, like he hadn't slept well in weeks. And his hands... his hands were gentle. Careful. The way he handled the bow made me think he understood things most people didn't.

But what caught me wasn't how he looked. It was the feeling.

He looked... hollow. Like something had been scraped out of him and he was pretending not to notice.

I knew that feeling.

The previous night, my little sister had cried herself to sleep because she missed a father who hadn't earned the right to be missed. I'd sat with her, rubbing her back, telling her stories until her breathing evened. Then I'd gone to my room and practiced cello until my fingers ached, trying to drown the same ache that lived in me.

So yes — I knew that look.

The hollow one.

Only on him, it looked like it ran deeper.

…f…

"Everyone check your rosin," Mrs. Dalton called from her podium.

Almost immediately, there was a groan from the cello section.

"Uh—mine's gone," someone said.

It was him.

His voice was soft. Rough around the edges.

Our eyes met again.

Before I could stop myself, I said, "I have extra."

His brows lifted slightly, surprised.

I reached into my bag and handed him my spare rosin. "Here. You can borrow it."

He hesitated — not because he didn't want to take it, but because he seemed unsure he deserved anyone's help.

"Thanks," he murmured, touching the amber block like it might break.

"You're welcome," I whispered.

He held my gaze a heartbeat longer than before, and this time he didn't look away immediately. There was something almost vulnerable in his eyes, like he was waiting to be judged and didn't know what to do with the fact that I wasn't judging him at all.

And then the moment passed.

Mrs. Dalton tapped her baton, and we launched into warmups.

…ƒ…

When he played his first note, I actually stopped.

It wasn't that he was perfect. He wasn't. His intonation wavered on the shift, his bow trembled slightly on the downstroke.

But the emotion in his playing — the honesty — it was like he poured something raw into every note.

People don't play like that unless they've lived through something that left a mark.

While the rest of the room chattered, he played quietly. Barely loud enough for the section to hear. But I heard him. Every note felt like a story without words. I found myself mirroring his bowing instinctively, trying to match the way he breathed through the phrases.

Halfway through rehearsal, Mrs. Dalton paired section members for bowing checks.

Before I could move, he stood and walked toward me.

"Do you want to check?" he asked softly.

His eyes flicked to mine, then dropped to the floor like he regretted asking.

I nodded. "Yeah. Sure."

We sat close together, our chairs nearly touching. I noticed he smelled faintly like clean laundry and something I couldn't name — sadness, maybe. But there was a warmth under it too.

We leaned over the same sheet of music, elbows brushing.

"That eighth-note run always gets me," he admitted, tapping the page. "Feels like it's running away from me."

I smiled. "It's not running. It's just… anxious."

42

He gave a small laugh — soft, startled — like he hadn't expected anyone to respond that way.

"You're Rose, right?" he asked.

"Yes."

"I'm Gabriel."

Gabriel.

I'd heard the name around school. Whispers. Glances. Nothing concrete. Just an unspoken sense that people understood something about him that he didn't say aloud.

His fingers brushed mine as he adjusted the music stand, and he muttered, "Sorry."

"It's okay," I whispered. But it wasn't just okay. Something about the touch lingered, like the warmth of a candle after the flame goes out.

We started the passage, our bows rising and falling together. And for a moment — just a moment — everything felt aligned. Like our breathing matched. Like the music tethered us to the same place.

He played the shift cleanly this time. He didn't notice he'd done it right. But I did.

When rehearsal ended, he handed the rosin back to me with that same hesitant gentleness.

"Thanks again," he murmured.

"Anytime," I said. And I meant it.

As he walked away, he glanced back once — a quick, uncertain flick of his eyes, like he was checking to see if I was still real.

I was.

And something in me knew I would keep noticing him. Not

because of how he looked. Not because of how he played. But because of that hollow space inside him that felt too familiar.

The world didn't slow down when I met Gabriel. It didn't tilt or shimmer or ring with music.

But something small inside me — something quiet and careful — shifted toward him. Like a string tuning itself to the right pitch.

I didn't know it yet. But that was the beginning.

The first light.

The moment my story found its way toward his.

CHAPTER 7
ROSE

Falling Slowly

After that first day, something started happening that I couldn't explain. I found myself looking for Gabriel without meaning to. In the hallway between classes. Across the orchestra room. In the cafeteria line. Not in the obvious, movie-version way, where a girl stares dramatically and blushes when he looks over. This was quieter.

Like my eyes knew where he was before my mind thought to check.

He didn't look at me often. But when he did, it was always quick — almost shy — and something in me warmed in a way that felt dangerous.

Not dangerous like fire. Dangerous like hope.

During our next rehearsal, Mrs. Dalton announced that we'd be pairing for the winter concert duet rotations. My pulse jumped in my throat. I tried not to look at Gabriel. I tried even harder not to hope.

But when she called our names together — "Gabriel and Rose for Rotation Three" — my stomach fluttered like someone had snapped a bow across my ribs.

He glanced at me, a small, surprised half-smile tugging at the corner of his mouth. Not the sad smile. Not the polite one.

A real one.

We spent the next several days practicing after school in one of the tiny practice rooms. It was barely big enough for two chairs and a stand, but somehow it felt like a world of its own — warm, dusty, filled with the soft hum of old carpet and spent resin.

At first, we barely talked.

We'd sit close, shoulders brushing when we leaned in to mark fingerings. His hands moved carefully across the cello strings, as if he were afraid of hurting them. Sometimes I'd catch his breath stuttering on difficult passages, and he'd shake his head, embarrassed.

"It's okay," I'd say gently. "Try it slower."

He'd nod, eyes dropping, and repeat the measure. When he got it right — when something clicked — he didn't celebrate or grin or look proud.

He just looked relieved.

As if success wasn't joy. Just temporary safety.

That was one of the first things I learned about him.

He didn't know how to accept being good at something.

…f…

One afternoon after practice, he gathered up his music

sheets and hesitated before putting them in his bag.

"Can I ask you something?" he said softly.

"Of course."

He rubbed the back of his neck. "Am I... messing you up? When we play?"

"No," I said too quickly. Then softer, "Not at all. You're good, Gabriel."

He blinked like I'd spoken in another language.

"Thanks," he said, eyes dropping as he zipped his bag.

That was it. That was the whole conversation.

But the way he said "thanks" stayed with me all night — like no one said it to him often. Or like he didn't believe them when they did.

…♩…

A week later, we had one of the easiest days I'd ever seen from him.

It happened during lunch, outside in the courtyard where the sun warmed the stone benches. Autumn and Marilyn were arguing about whether Coldplay was "genius or lullaby music," trading jabs and laughing. I sat between them, picking at my sandwich, when Gabriel wandered up and sat on the bench beside me like it was the most natural thing in the world.

"Hey," he said quietly.

My heartbeat quickened. "Hi."

Autumn grinned. Marilyn raised an eyebrow that I pretended not to notice.

We talked about nothing — school, orchestra, the calc teacher who always smelled like oranges. Gabriel said something sarcastic under his breath about Autumn's sunglasses being "aggressively shiny," and she shoved him lightly, laughing. He grinned — really grinned — and some color returned to his face I hadn't seen before.

For a moment, he looked like a boy who didn't have shadows in his eyes.

We started looping the courtyard after eating — just walking and talking, Marilyn tossing bits of leaves at him, Autumn teasing, the four of us drifting into a rhythm that felt easy.

When he walked next to me, he kept just barely brushing my arm with his.

Not enough for anyone to comment.

Just enough for me to feel.

The courtyard loop became a habit — one he joined more days than not. Some days he was talkative. Some days quiet. Once, he surprised me by asking if I liked Anne Rice, because he'd overheard me mention an interview of hers in English.

I told him I loved her books. He smiled softly and said, "I figured you were the type."

I didn't know what that meant — not exactly — but the way he said it made warmth bloom in my chest.

…ƒ…

One Friday afternoon, when my sister needed help babysitting, I brought my nephews to the school after a rehearsal so she could pick them up. They clung to my legs, giggling and asking if the instruments "made magic."

Gabriel walked up with his cello case slung over his shoulder.

He froze when he saw the boys, uncertainty flickering across his face — like he wasn't sure how to exist around small children. But Rowan, the older one, marched right up and poked the case.

"What's that?"

Gabriel blinked. "It's a… cello."

"Does it roar?" Rowan asked.

Gabriel laughed — really laughed — and knelt to unzip the top enough to show the neck.

"No roaring. Just music."

Rowan touched the strings with two fingers like he was petting a dragon. Gabriel didn't flinch. He actually lowered the case so Rowan could see better.

"You're… good at that," I said quietly once the boys ran off.

He shrugged, cheeks pink. "Kids are easier than people."

I smiled. "You're good with people too."

He looked away quickly, the color in his cheeks deepening.

…ƒ…

Little by little, I felt myself leaning toward him. Not all at once. Not with dramatic declarations.

Just… slowly.

At the end of each school day, I'd catch myself hoping he'd walk through the courtyard at the same time I did. When the bell rang, I'd hear his laugh before I saw him. During class, I'd glance up during tuning and find him already looking at me, then looking away fast, like he hadn't meant to.

I wasn't falling fast. I wasn't falling blindly.

49

I was falling *softly*.

Into the spaces between his silences. Into the gentleness he didn't think anyone could see. Into the good parts that flickered like candlelight under everything he tried to hide.

I didn't know yet how fragile he really was. How deep the cracks went. How much I'd wish I could go back and protect him from himself.

All I knew was that when Gabriel smiled — the real smile — I felt something inside me unfold. Something warm. Something hopeful.

And it scared me a little.

Because hope, once you have it, is the hardest thing to let go.

CHAPTER 8
ROSE

Becoming Us

There was not one single day when we became a couple. No dramatic announcement. No "Will you be my girlfriend?" typed out in a text with too many emojis. It happened the way weather does in West Texas — slowly, quietly, and then all at once.

One day we were walking the courtyard loop with Autumn and Marilyn. A few weeks later, we were walking it just the two of us.

It started with small things. Little shifts that almost did not register until I looked back and realized how far we had moved.

He stopped sitting across from me at lunch and started sitting beside me. He stopped saying "see you around" and started saying "see you tomorrow." He started waiting in the hallway outside my last class of the day without being asked.

"I'm not stalking you," he said once, hands in his pockets,

cheeks flushed. "I just… happen to be here when the bell rings."

"Convenient timing," I teased.

"Very," he said, and the way he looked at me made my stomach flutter.

On Saturdays, I started showing up at his house "for practice," even when we did not really practice. We'd play through our orchestra pieces once or twice, then drift into other things — movie soundtracks, sad piano pieces arranged for strings, songs he liked that I tried to figure out by ear. His parents were almost always kind. His mom would offer me something to drink. His dad would ask about school and joke about musicians being "the sensitive ones."

They both looked at me like they were glad I was there.

I did not realize how starved I was for that feeling until I felt it.

At home, I was needed. At Gabriel's, I was wanted.

Somewhere in all of that, lines blurred without either of us saying they had.

…f…

The first time I realized other people saw it before we did was in the lunch line. Autumn stepped behind me, dropped her tray down on the rail with a clatter, and nodded toward Gabriel, who was leaning against the far wall, waiting.

"You know he only stands there for you, right?" she said.

I rolled my eyes. "He's just waiting for lunch."

"For *you*," she repeated. "He checks the clock for *your* class. He doesn't stand there when you're sick."

"How do you even know that?"

"I notice things," she said. "Like the way he looks at you when you talk and the rest of the room disappears."

My face grew warm. "You're being dramatic."

"You like him," she singsonged under her breath.

"I like a lot of people."

"Not like that."

I grabbed my tray and stepped forward before she could press more. But when I looked up, I caught Gabriel watching me the way Autumn had described — like the rest of the line, the noise, the fluorescent lights were blurred out and I was the only thing in focus.

I felt that same dangerous, gentle tug in my chest.

I liked him. I knew that.

But it was starting to feel bigger than like.

…f…

A few weeks later, my nephews came over while I was getting ready to go to his house. They climbed onto my bed, knocking over my sheet music, asking a thousand questions at once.

"Are you going to see the music boy?" Rowan asked, mispronouncing his name in the way only he could.

"His name is Gabriel," I corrected, trying not to smile too hard.

"Do you love him?" the younger one blurted.

I froze halfway through tying my shoe. "What?"

"Mommy said you're always at his house," he added matter-of-factly. "That means you love him, right?"

"Mommy needs to stop talking about me," I muttered.

They stared, waiting.

I thought about Gabriel's laugh. The way he softened

53

around my nephews. The way he always asked if I'd eaten. The way he listened to me talk about Anne Rice and actually cared. The way he seemed surprised every time I chose to stay.

"I care about him," I said finally.

"That means yes," Rowan declared, rolling off the bed.

I did not confirm. I did not deny. I just finished tying my shoes and tried to ignore how accurate a six-year-old could be.

…f…

The first kiss happened on a Tuesday.

Not a special day. Not a Friday night. Just a regular evening where homework and fatigue hung in the air.

We were sitting on his living room floor, backs against the couch, a bowl of popcorn between us and some movie playing we were not really watching. His parents had gone to bed early. The house was dark except for the glow of the TV.

He was quiet. Too quiet.

"Are you okay?" I asked, turning slightly toward him.

"Yeah," he said, but his voice sounded thin.

"Liar."

He smiled faintly. "You're getting good at catching that."

"I have a lot of practice," I said softly.

He looked down at his hands, fingers picking at a loose thread on the couch cushion. "Do you ever feel like… if people really knew you, they'd leave?"

The question landed in my chest with a familiar thud.

"Yes," I said, without joking or deflecting. "All the time."

He looked up sharply, studying my face like he was trying to see if I meant it.

"And yet," I added, "you're still here. And I'm still here. So maybe that fear lies to both of us."

He swallowed, throat working. "You don't know everything about me, Rose."

"I know enough to choose you," I said.

The words slipped out before I could edit them.

His eyes widened slightly. The room suddenly felt too quiet. Even the noise from the TV faded into the background.

"Choose me?" he repeated, barely above a whisper.

Heat crawled up my neck. "I mean— as a friend. As… as someone I care about."

He did not look away this time. He didn't smirk. He didn't deflect.

He just looked at me — long, searching — like he was memorizing my face.

My heart hammered so hard I could hear my pulse in my ears.

"I choose you too," he said.

The space between us felt very small after that. I became acutely aware of how close our shoulders were, how the side of his leg brushed mine, how his hand was resting, open-palmed, on the carpet near my own.

I could have moved away. I did not.

Slowly, as if afraid of startling me, he turned his hand so that his fingertips touched mine. A question, not a demand.

I answered without words.

I turned my hand and threaded my fingers through his.

His breath hitched. Mine did too.

We stayed like that for a long time, saying nothing, just sharing the same space, the same air, the same racing heartbeat.

When he finally leaned in, it was not sudden. It was hesitant. Careful.

He shifted closer, eyes flicking down to my mouth and back up to my eyes, silently asking for permission.

I nodded before I could think better of it.

His lips brushed mine — soft, trembling, almost cautious.

My entire body went still.

It wasn't fireworks. It wasn't cinematic. It was something quieter and somehow more dangerous — like being handed something fragile and realizing you wanted to spend a very long time protecting it.

He pulled back an inch, searching my face. "Was that… okay?"

I let out a breath I did not realize I had been holding. "Yes."

"Are you sure? Because if it wasn't—"

"It was," I said, louder this time.

He smiled, a little crooked, a little disbelieving. "Okay."

We leaned in again. The second kiss was a little less shaky. A little more real. A little more *us*.

When we finally separated, we did not move far. Our foreheads rested together, breaths mingling.

"Does this mean…?" he started, then trailed off.

I knew what he was trying to ask. The words felt heavy in my mouth.

"If you're asking whether we're a 'thing' now," I said gently, "I'd like to be. With you."

He exhaled a shaky laugh. "Yeah. Me too."

A warmth settled in my sternum, deep and steady. It felt like the beginning of something. And in a way, it was.

…ƒ…

After that night, nothing in our schedule officially changed, but everything in us did.

People at school noticed. They always do.

Gabriel and I walked together more. He met me at my locker. I found notes folded into my sheet music in his messy handwriting — stupid doodles, half-finished lyrics, "good luck" scrawled before a test.

Autumn started calling us "an old married couple" when we bickered playfully about tempo. Marilyn just smiled a quiet, knowing smile that said she'd seen this coming for a long time.

By spring, people had started saying our names like one word. RoseandGabriel. Not separate. Not divided.

On weekends, I was at his house so often my sisters joked about forwarding my mail there. His mom kept my favorite cereal in the pantry "just in case." His dad asked my opinion on which movies to rent. It felt… real. Solid. Like we were building something together.

Of course, I knew things were not perfect inside him. I saw the days when his eyes went distant, when his laugh dimmed, when he flinched at shadows I could not see.

But I also saw the good. The boy who picked up dropped books for strangers. The boy who let my nephews climb all over him. The boy who played cello like it was the only honest language he had left.

I saw all of it.

And as the days warmed and the year leaned toward summer, one truth settled deeper and deeper into my bones:

I was in love with Gabriel. Not the idea of him. Not the version people whispered about.

Him.

As he was. Broken places and all.

I did not know yet how much that love would cost. I did not know how sharp the edges of his pain really were.

Right then, under the early spring sun and the glow of cafeteria lights and the soft warmth of his living room, all I knew was this:

For the first time in a very long time, I felt chosen. And I was choosing him right back.

CHAPTER 9
ROSE

First Time

The night it happened didn't feel like a decision. Not a planned one, at least. It felt like the end of a thought neither of us had dared to say aloud.

It was early spring — the kind where the evenings still carried winter's breath but the days warmed enough to pretend it was almost summer. His house felt quiet that night, softer somehow. His parents had gone to bed early, and the living room lamp was the only light on, glowing like a warm little planet in the center of the room.

We were supposed to be watching a movie. I don't remember which one. I don't think either of us were really watching.

He sat on the floor again, leaning his back against the couch. I sat beside him, close enough that our knees brushed every time one of us shifted. He kept playing absently with the hem of his sleeve — tugging, twisting, releasing — like he was trying to work out some thought he couldn't say.

I could feel his tension before he spoke. Gabriel's moods always lived in the air around him.

"Rose?" he asked quietly.

"Yeah?"

He stared straight ahead, eyes fixed on the TV but not seeing it at all. "Do you ever feel like sometimes… you finally have something good, and it scares you?"

My breath stilled. "Yeah," I whispered. "I feel that."

"Sometimes I think—" He swallowed. "I think I'm going to mess this up. Us. You."

"You haven't," I said. "You won't."

He let out a shaky breath, like he wanted to believe me but didn't know how.

"We don't have to talk about this right now," I said gently. "We can just be here."

He nodded, eyes dropping to his hands again. "Being here with you is the easiest thing in my life."

That sentence landed somewhere deep in me — a place that feared love and longed for it in equal measure.

I moved my hand toward his slowly. He noticed. He looked at me. Really looked.

And the fear in his eyes softened — not gone, but quieter — like something inside him unclenched.

He turned toward me, lifting a hand to tuck a strand of hair behind my ear. His fingers trembled a little. Mine did too. There was something so vulnerable in that touch — as if he was asking permission without using words.

I leaned into his palm.

That was all it took.

He kissed me first — gentle, searching, unsure. Nothing rushed. Nothing hungry. Just careful, warm, real.

I kissed him back, and the world narrowed into the small space between us. The TV kept playing. The house stayed quiet. But everything in me felt bright and terrifying and right.

When we pulled back, his forehead rested against mine.

"I love you," he whispered, so softly I almost didn't hear it. Not dramatic. Not staged. Not pressured.

A truth slipping out of him.

My whole chest tightened. "I love you too," I breathed.

He closed his eyes, like he needed a moment to steady himself. Then he whispered:

"Come with me."

He stood and held out his hand — hesitant, hopeful, shaking slightly. I took it.

We climbed the stairs quietly. His room felt smaller than usual, warmer somehow. He closed the door but didn't lock it. The lamp on his dresser cast soft gold across his walls, and for a long moment we just stood there, holding hands, breathing in the same rhythm.

He touched my cheek again, slower this time. I lifted my hand and covered his.

Neither of us rushed. We moved like people trying not to break something sacred.

And when we finally crossed that line — when closeness became something deeper — it wasn't sudden. It wasn't dramatic.

It was gentle. Careful. Kind. A moment we built together, not something taken or forced.

When it became too much — too new, too vulnerable — he paused.

"Are you okay?" he whispered.

"Yes," I said.

"Are you sure? Because—"

"I'm sure."

I placed my hand against his chest. His heart was racing. So was mine.

He kissed me again, and everything after that felt like soft light. Warmth. Quiet breaths. Two people choosing each other in the only way they knew how at that age — with trembling hands and whole hearts.

And when it was over, we didn't talk right away. We lay there, wrapped in the same blanket, his arm around me, my head on his chest, listening to his heartbeat slow back down.

He whispered, "I've never done this before."

"Me neither," I said.

"Did I...? Was it...?" His voice cracked a little.

"It was us," I whispered. "That's enough."

He exhaled like he'd been holding his breath for years.

We stayed like that until his eyes grew heavy. I watched him fall asleep — the soft rise and fall of his chest, the small line between his eyebrows relaxing for the first time in months.

And I thought:

This is what he looks like when he feels safe. This is the boy beneath everything else. This is Gabriel.

I didn't know how fragile he still was. I didn't know how soon the world would break us open.

Right then, all I felt was warmth. And love. And the quiet certainty that this moment would stay with me forever.

CHAPTER 10
ROSE

The Freak Moment

The night air felt cooler than it should have for early summer. Not cold, exactly — just enough to brush goosebumps up my arms as we walked out of the rec center. The parking lot lights flickered overhead, casting long pale beams across the pavement. Gabriel jogged ahead a few feet and hopped up to sit on the hood of his truck, patting the space beside him without looking directly at me.

I slid up next to him, legs dangling over the bumper, shoulder just barely touching his. It felt like a familiar place — the two of us under the sky, pretending the world was simpler than it was.

He leaned back on his hands and exhaled slowly. Something in that exhale told me this wasn't just a casual end-of-the-night moment. Something was brewing in him.

"Rodney's a freak," he muttered suddenly.

The words dropped hard, like he'd been carrying them for hours and couldn't hold them anymore.

I blinked. "What?"

"Rodney," he repeated. "He's a freak… he's gay."

The way he said it — sharp, bitter — startled me. Not because of the word itself, but because of the *pain* under it. He wasn't talking about Rodney. He was talking about himself. I felt it immediately, like a string tightening between us.

Before I could respond, he went on, staring straight ahead, voice low and cracking at the edges.

"There are other freak things, too. Stuff that makes you… not normal."

My heart pulled tight in my chest.

There it is. The thing I'd felt in him for months. The heaviness. The hidden shame. The way he sometimes looked at the ground instead of at me.

He was trembling, just barely — in the jaw, in the hands, in the breath.

I kept my voice soft. "Such as?"

He closed his eyes. His throat bobbed with a swallow that looked like it hurt. When he spoke again, his voice was small. Raw.

"I'm a freak too."

I didn't breathe for a moment. Not out of shock — out of heartbreak.

He said it like a confession. Like he was waiting for me to flinch. To pull away. To nod in agreement. To confirm the thing he feared most.

And I realized — suddenly, painfully — that he wasn't asking for validation. He was bracing for rejection.

My father's voice flashed in the back of my mind — the way he'd used scripture like accusation, like shame, like a cage. The way he'd taught me to fear certain words, certain people, certain wounds.

I swallowed hard.

I could not let Gabriel face that alone.

He looked at me then — really looked — his eyes wet and frantic in the glow of the parking lot lights.

And I knew what he saw in that moment would shape him.

The wrong answer would break him. Silence would break him. Arguing would break him.

I had one job. To keep him from falling apart in front of me.

So I smiled — a small, trembling thing — not because I believed what I was about to say, but because I knew *he* needed it.

"I'm a freak too," I whispered.

His breath caught.

Relief washed over him so fast it looked like he might collapse. He didn't. He just stared at me with this stunned, grateful softness — the kind that said he'd been holding his breath for years and finally let a piece of it go.

He believed me.

Of course he did.

He needed to.

And I wanted — with every fragile, aching part of me — to be whatever made him feel less alone.

He leaned in and kissed me — slow, desperate, clinging.

Not passionate. More like he needed to hold onto something before it blew away.

I kissed him back. Not out of obligation. Out of love.

Because no one had ever trusted me with their wounds the way he was right then.

…ƒ…

Later, when I got home, the truth hit me differently.

I sat on my bed with the lights off, the window cracked open for air. My fingers pressed into my knees, my heart still pounding.

"I'm a freak too."

The words replayed in my head, echoing with a guilt I hadn't felt in the moment.

Because I wasn't. Not in the way he meant. He had meant something deeper, darker — something tied to shame he carried like a stone in his chest.

He was asking, "Will you still love me if I am broken?" And I had answered, "I'll be broken with you."

I wasn't lying. But I wasn't telling the truth either.

I wasn't calling myself a freak. I was telling him he wasn't one.

Or at least, that if he was — he wasn't alone there.

And that was what he needed.

Even if it left a small crack inside me.

A place where I knew I had stepped into his pain instead of pulling him into my light.

I lay back on my pillow, staring at the ceiling, my throat tight.

I loved him. I loved him in a way that scared me. Enough

68

to say words I didn't believe just to hold him together for one more night under the stars.

The freak moment wasn't about me. It was about him.

The boy who thought he was unlovable. The boy who thought he was wrong. The boy who believed the word freak belonged to him.

And the girl who didn't know how to tell him that he was the furthest thing from it she had ever known.

CHAPTER 11
ROSE

Weekend Setup

The night that would unravel everything didn't begin with tension. It began with a mall.

A stupid, ordinary mall filled with stale popcorn, giggling middle-schoolers, and the hum of conversation bouncing off tile floors. We had gone with Clay and Amber because Amber wanted to "wand-pretend shop," which was her dramatic way of saying she wanted to walk around holding a drink and judging people's outfits.

I told myself I was going for fun. For the distraction. For Gabriel.

But if I'm honest, I went because he asked me to. Even though something in him already felt… off.

Not enough to name. Just enough to notice.

He'd been quieter the whole week leading up to it — his eyes distant during orchestra, fingers tapping anxiously on his knee during lunch, shoulders curled inward like he was bracing for something he couldn't dodge.

Whenever I asked what was wrong, he said "nothing." And I wanted to believe him. But the lie sat badly in my chest.

That night at the mall, he stayed close — too close for a place that bright and crowded. Every so often, he brushed his knuckles against mine like he needed to check if I was still there. I squeezed his hand once, gently, hoping he'd feel anchored.

His smile didn't quite reach his eyes.

…ƒ…

The four of us drifted in and out of stores, Clay making sarcastic comments about overpriced shoes, Amber trying on sunglasses and asking which pair made her look "like an unapproachable goddess." I laughed when I was supposed to. I leaned against Gabriel's shoulder when he leaned into mine.

But something in him wasn't settling.

It felt like trying to hold someone during an earthquake — the tremors too small to panic, too steady to ignore.

At one point, in the food court line, I tugged lightly on his sleeve.

"You okay?"

He nodded. Too quickly. Too practiced.

72

"I'm good."

I didn't push. I should have. But I didn't.

Because that week — and especially that night — he was fragile in a way I didn't understand yet, and I didn't want to crack him open by accident.

···f···

We ended up in the board game shop because Clay wanted to find something "not boring for once." Amber trailed behind, looking bored already.

Then she spotted it — a clear plastic container with a twenty-sided die sitting inside.

"Oh my gosh," she said, grabbing it dramatically. "This. We're getting this."

Clay groaned. "Why? What do we need dice for?"

Amber wiggled the container in front of him. "Because this, my sweet idiot boyfriend, will decide what we do tonight."

I laughed. "That's actually kind of fun."

Gabriel stayed quiet, shifting on his feet, watching Amber the way someone watches a lit match too close to fabric. His jaw tensed when she shook the die and said, "High numbers mean risky."

He glanced at me, something warning-shaped in his eyes.

I thought: *We'll be fine. It's a game.*

I was wrong. But I didn't know that yet.

73

After the mall, we split into our usual boy-girl pairings. Clay drove with Amber. I rode with Gabriel.

As soon as we got into his truck, he rested his forehead against the steering wheel and exhaled hard.

"Gabriel… talk to me."

"I'm fine." Familiar. Automatic.

I touched his arm. He flinched — not away from me, but like a jolt went through him.

"You're not fine," I whispered.

He swallowed, eyes closing. "Just… stay close tonight, okay?"

Something cold brushed down my spine.

"Why?"

He didn't answer.

Instead, he reached over and took my hand — squeezing it a fraction too tight — as if he could already feel something slipping.

As if he knew what I didn't.

As if the dice weren't a game at all.

At his house, before Clay and Amber arrived, we sat on the edge of his bed. His room was dim, only the small lamp on. His hand stayed in mine the whole time, thumb brushing the inside of my wrist like he was memorizing my pulse.

"Gabriel," I tried again softly, "whatever is bothering

you, you can tell me."

"I know," he whispered. But he still didn't.

He kissed my forehead. Soft. Almost apologetic.

Then he stood when he heard the knock downstairs, shoulders stiffening as if bracing for impact.

…*f*…

Amber burst through the front door, already waving the die.

"Okay, losers," she said, laughing. "The night begins!"

Gabriel's jaw twitched.

Clay snorted. "It's a stupid game, man."

A tiny muscle in Gabriel's cheek moved. "Yeah. Stupid."

His voice was calm. Too calm.

I felt something in my stomach tighten.

He led us upstairs to his room. Amber dumped her bag onto the floor. Clay kicked off his shoes. Everyone shrugged off the weight of the evening like it was nothing.

But Gabriel stayed close to me. Too close. The way people stand near fire when they're afraid of the dark.

I should have seen it. I should have named it. I should have said, "Let's not do this."

But I was seventeen, in love, and believing things would always be okay if we stayed together in the same room.

And he was eighteen, carrying a storm I didn't know how to read yet.

75

Amber rattled the die in the container, grinning wickedly.

"Let's play."

Gabriel flinched. Barely noticeable. But I saw it.

His hand found mine under the blanket of blankets we'd gathered on the floor.

His grip said everything his voice didn't.

Stay with me. Don't leave me alone in this. I need you.

I squeezed back.

I had no idea how wrong things were about to go. No way of knowing how fast the night would splinter. Or how deeply it would change everything that came after.

All I knew was that I loved him. And that the die, sitting innocently in Amber's hand, was about to drop into a story I wasn't ready for.

CHAPTER 12
ROSE

The Breaking

The night didn't collapse quickly. It sagged first — like something buckling under weight we didn't notice until it was too late.

We were on Gabriel's bedroom floor, legs crossed, backs against the bed or the wall, everyone pretending we were still just kids playing a stupid game. Amber rattled the die in its plastic cup like she was auditioning for a role in chaos.

Her turn came again. She rolled. She read the dare. And her face tightened.

"Nope," she said immediately, standing. "Not doing that."

Clay laughed. "Oh, come on—"

"No," she snapped. "Game's dumb anyway."

She grabbed her bag, shoved past Gabriel's doorway, and stomped down the hall. A moment later, the front door slammed.

And then it was only three of us. Me. Clay. Gabriel.

The room seemed to shrink.

Clay looked uncomfortable for the first time all night. He shifted on the floor, scratched the back of his neck, then forced a laugh.

"So… guess it's my turn again."

Gabriel didn't laugh. He didn't smile. He didn't move.

He just stared at the die like he already knew something terrible was sitting inside it.

Clay rolled.

Amber wasn't there to read it. So Clay did. And whatever he saw in that little circle of numbers made his cheeks color with something like embarrassment — and something like dread.

"Seriously?" he muttered under his breath.

He looked at Gabriel. Not at me.

Something unspoken passed between the two of them, something I didn't have the language for at seventeen.

Gabriel exhaled — long, shaky — like a man bracing for impact.

He stood. Clay stood too. Neither of them said a word.

Gabriel didn't look at me. Clay didn't either.

Clay glanced toward the hallway.

Gabriel followed.

And they disappeared into the next room.

The door closed.

The house went silent.

…ƒ…

At first, I thought they were talking. Arguing quietly.

Sorting out some weird dare-boy-stupidity I would never fully understand.

But then the silence stretched. Too long. Too still.

And then—

A sound.

Small. Muted. Not clear.

But enough.

Enough to know something was happening that shouldn't be. Something private. Something wrong. Something I didn't understand.

My stomach churned. My breath stuttered. My hands went cold.

I wanted to knock on the wall. I wanted to yell. I wanted to demand an explanation.

But shock held me in place.

I sat on Gabriel's bed because my legs wouldn't hold me. Hands in my lap. Head bowed. Listening to something I didn't want to hear.

Not because I wanted to. Because I couldn't *not*.

And something inside me began to break.

Not loudly. Not even visibly. Just… quietly.

Quiet enough that only the walls could hear it.

…ƒ…

When the sound finally stopped, I didn't breathe.

Footsteps. Soft. Uneven.

Clay left first.

He didn't look at me. He didn't look at Gabriel.

He just walked out — out the bedroom, down the hall, out

the house — like he couldn't escape fast enough.

The front door clicked shut behind him.

And then there was nothing.

Just silence.

Deep. Hollow. Wrong.

I covered my mouth with both hands, but the sob escaped anyway — a small, broken sound I didn't mean to let out.

I pressed harder against my lips.

Be quiet. Don't let him hear. Don't let him see what this did to you.

But grief doesn't listen to commands.

The next sob came despite me — soft, shaking, bleeding into the walls the same way his pain had bled into the air all night.

My tears hit my palms. My breath stuttered. My shoulders shook, though I tried to hold perfectly still.

I didn't understand everything that had happened in that other room. But I understood enough. Enough to feel sick. Enough to feel betrayed and terrified and heartbreakingly sad. Not just for myself.

For him.

Because whatever happened — whatever line Clay and Gabriel had crossed — it wasn't about desire. It wasn't curiosity. It wasn't teenage stupidity.

It was pain. A pain Gabriel recognized before it happened. A pain he couldn't stop. A pain he had already lived once.

And now I had lived a shadow of it too — as a witness, not a participant — and even that was enough to crack something in me.

…f…

A soft creak made me look up.

Gabriel stood in the doorway of the hall, silhouette outlined by the dim light.

He looked… destroyed.

Not guilty. Not ashamed in the way I expected. Just —

Destroyed.

Like something inside him had collapsed under the weight of what he thought he deserved.

He stepped toward me slowly, as if afraid I'd pull away.

I didn't.

I couldn't.

He didn't speak. I couldn't either.

He sat on the floor at my feet and rested his forehead against my knee — not asking for forgiveness, not defending himself, not explaining, not even breathing steadily.

Just existing there. Near me. Broken beside my breaking.

And I put a trembling hand in his hair because I didn't know what else to do.

My voice didn't work. My heart did.

We stayed like that a long time — two kids in the half-dark, carrying wounds neither of us had the strength to name.

And even then —

Even through all the hurt and confusion and fear —

I loved him.

That was the worst part.

That I loved him.

And that I did not know how much this night would cost both of us.

CHAPTER 13
ROSE & MARILYN

Silent Treaty

The first school day after *that* night, everything felt too bright.

Rose

The sun coming through my bedroom window was rude. It cut across my pillow as if nothing had happened, as if the world had not bent sideways in Gabriel's house and left me standing at the edge of something I did not have words for.

I got dressed on autopilot. Jeans. T-shirt. Hoodie, even though it would be too warm by lunch. It felt like armor. Something to hide inside.

My sisters asked normal questions. "Can you braid my hair?" "Have you seen my shoes?" "Are you going to be home for dinner?"

I answered them all. "Yes." "By the door." "I don't know

yet."

My voice sounded distant in my own ears, like I was listening to someone else speaking.

On the drive to school, my mom talked about bills and groceries and whether we needed to cut back on eating out. I nodded at the right moments, but my brain was still in that house. Still on that bed. Still hearing the quiet, awful silence in the next room.

I had not talked to Gabriel since.

He had texted once.

Are you okay?

I read it. Stared at it until the screen dimmed. Then set my phone face-down and pretended I did not feel like I was choking.

Because the truth? I did not know if I was okay. And I definitely did not know if he was.

I stepped out of the car, adjusted my backpack, and did the thing I had always done — I kept walking.

If I stopped, I was afraid everything inside me would spill out in the middle of the parking lot.

…ƒ…

Marilyn

I spotted her before she saw me.

I was leaning against the brick wall near the side entrance, watching students pour in — the usual Monday sea of tired faces and half-zipped backpacks — when Rose stepped out of her mom's car.

Normally she walked with this quiet kind of purpose. Not loud, not bouncy, just steady. Today, she moved like someone trying not to wake a sleeping monster. Every step careful. Shoulders tight. Eyes down.

My chest tightened.

Something had happened.

I had not heard from Gabriel all weekend either. That alone was strange. But this? Rose looking like a ghost in broad daylight?

That scared me.

I pushed off the wall and started toward her.

She did not see me at first. Her gaze was glued to the pavement, like if she met anyone's eyes they might see everything she was trying to keep hidden.

"Hey," I said softly when I reached her.

She flinched, just a little, then forced a smile that did not even try to reach her eyes. "Hey."

Up close, I could see it — the faint swelling around her eyelids, the tight set of her mouth, the way she held her shoulders as if bracing for impact.

"You look tired," I said.

It was the gentlest thing I could think of that was also true.

She nodded. "Didn't sleep much."

I wanted to ask why. I didn't. I had grown up with my own silences. You learn to recognize when someone is wrapped in a kind of quiet that questions can't fix.

"Come on," I said, angling my body slightly toward the side of the building. "Bell's going to ring. We can cut the crowd if we go around."

She followed.

We walked side by side — not touching, not talking — and I could feel the weight hanging between us. I suspected it had a name.

Gabriel.

…*f*…

Rose

I knew Marilyn was watching me without looking directly at me. That was one of the things I liked about her. She noticed something was wrong and stayed close without poking at the wound.

We slipped through a less crowded side door and made our way toward the orchestra room. Every step closer made my stomach turn.

Because I knew who would be there. Because I knew I would have to see him. Because I did not know what my face would do when I did.

"Do you want to skip first period?" Marilyn asked quietly as we walked. "We could hide in the library."

Part of me wanted to say yes. To vanish into the rows of shelves and pretend the rest of the world did not exist.

But the other part — the stubborn, loyal part — knew I had not decided anything yet. About Gabriel. About us. About what the night meant.

"I have a quiz," I said. It was not entirely a lie. "I'll be okay."

She didn't argue, but I saw her jaw tighten slightly, like she knew "okay" was doing a lot of work in that sentence.

When we pushed open the orchestra room door, my heart started pounding so hard I wondered if she could hear it.

He was there.

86

Of course he was.

Sitting in his usual chair in the cello section, case open, bow in hand. He looked... wrecked. Pale. Eyes ringed with sleeplessness. Hands hovering over the strings like he wasn't sure they'd respond.

For a second, our eyes almost met.

Almost.

I turned away first.

Cowardly? Maybe. Necessary? Absolutely.

I moved toward my seat with Marilyn at my side, and I pretended I didn't feel Gabriel's gaze trying to find me in the background noise of tuning and chatter.

I focused on my music stand. On tightening my bow. On breathing in and out evenly.

I did not look at him.

Not once.

...f...

Marilyn

I saw it all.

The way Gabriel's face shifted when Rose walked in — hope first, then something like fear, then a softness I rarely saw in him unless she was around.

The way that softness shattered when she turned away.

He stared at the floor after that, fingers trembling slightly as he tightened his bow. He looked like he wanted to disappear into the chair.

I knew that look. I had seen it on him before. Just never with her involved.

I slid my chair closer to Rose's. Not dramatically. Just enough that our knees almost touched when we sat. A subtle signal.

I'm here. You're not alone. You don't have to look at him if you're not ready.

Mrs. Dalton started warm-ups. Bows rose and fell. Notes hummed through the room.

Rose's intonation was off at first — just barely, the tiniest wobble on the A — and no one else would have noticed, but I did. She was usually steady. Today, she was shaking.

In the middle of scales, I leaned a fraction toward her and whispered, "Breathe. You're okay."

She nodded without looking my way. Her shoulders dropped half an inch. Her tone steadied.

Across the room, Gabriel flinched at a missed shift and cursed under his breath. Mrs. Dalton didn't hear it. I did.

He kept glancing in our direction, but every time his eyes neared Rose, she stayed fixed on the music. On the conductor. On anything but him.

I felt torn clean in two.

I loved them both, differently. He was my almost-brother. She had become my friend.

And now there was a canyon between them, and I could not jump to both sides.

So I chose the side that looked more likely to collapse if I left it alone.

I chose Rose.

···*f*···

Rose

By lunchtime, I felt like I had run a marathon without moving more than fifty feet at a time. My brain was foggy. My body felt heavy. Every hallway looked too long.

I carried my tray toward the courtyard out of habit. That was where we always went — me, Autumn, Marilyn, Gabriel. Our little loop. Our little orbit.

Halfway there, my feet slowed.

I couldn't do it. Not today.

The thought of sitting at that table, pretending nothing had changed, pretending my chest wasn't full of broken glass, pretending the night at his house wasn't replaying in the back of my mind — it made my vision blur.

I stopped. Turned.

"Hey," Marilyn called behind me. "Courtyard's that way."

"I know," I said quietly. "I just… I think I'm going to eat inside today."

She studied me for a long second.

Then she nodded. "Okay."

I waited for her to walk away. She didn't.

"You don't have to follow me," I said, staring at the tray. "You can go with them."

"With who?" she asked.

"Autumn. Gabriel. Everyone."

"I am going with 'everyone,'" she replied.

When I looked up, she was already turning toward the side door that led into the quieter, empty wing near the practice rooms.

I followed silently.

We ended up sitting on the floor against a row of lockers,

our trays balanced on our knees. It wasn't glamorous. It wasn't our usual table. But it was away.

Away from Gabriel's eyes. Away from questions. Away from the version of me that did not know how to exist around him yet.

We ate in near-silence.

Halfway through a bite, my throat closed, and I set my sandwich down with shaking hands.

"Do you…" I started, then stopped.

Marilyn waited.

"Do you think…" I tried again, "people can do things that hurt you and still… be good?"

The words hung there between us.

She chewed slowly, swallowed, and took a breath.

"I think," she said carefully, "that people can be hurt in ways that make them hurt others. And I think that is complicated."

Complicated. That word felt safer than "evil." Less final than "unforgivable."

I stared at the linoleum and whispered, "I don't know what to do."

Marilyn's eyes softened. "You don't have to decide everything today."

"But—"

"Rose," she interrupted gently. "You're allowed to take time. To be confused. To be angry. To be sad. You don't owe anyone immediate clarity."

I swallowed, tears pressing at the backs of my eyes.

"I still…" My voice wobbled. "I still care about him."

"I know," she said. No judgment.

"And I feel terrible. And guilty. And mad. And—"

"I know that too."

Her certainty almost cracked me open.

I didn't say his name. She didn't say his name.

But we were talking about him. And we both knew it.

That was the treaty starting to form — a shared understanding that some things would never be fully said out loud, but neither of us would pretend they didn't exist.

…ƒ…

Marilyn

I didn't need Rose to explain what had happened.

I didn't know the details. Didn't want them. But I knew enough.

I'd heard the edges of it in Gabriel's voice when he answered my call Saturday afternoon — the way he sounded hollow and hoarse and apologetic without saying the words "I'm sorry." I'd felt it in the long stretches of silence where he didn't argue when I was angry and didn't defend himself when I asked, "What happened?"

He'd said only one clear sentence when I pushed too hard.

"I hurt her."

He hadn't meant in the physical sense. I could tell. He meant something deeper. Something knotted.

After that, he clammed up. I'd sworn at him. He took it.

Now, watching Rose pick at the crust of her sandwich, eyes glassy, I felt anger twist inside me in a way I wasn't used to.

Anger at him. Anger at whatever had twisted him long

91

before this. Anger at a world that could break a boy so badly that he didn't know how to stop breaking things around him.

But none of that anger was for her.

For her, I had only softness.

She looked so small, leaning her head back against the lockers, staring blankly at the ceiling as if answers might be hidden in the water stains.

"I feel like something's wrong with me," she said suddenly. "For still caring."

"Nothing is wrong with you," I said immediately.

She laughed once, without humor. "You're just saying that."

"No," I said, more firmly. "I'm not."

I set my tray aside and turned my body fully toward her.

"Listen," I said quietly. "Loving someone doesn't make you wrong. It doesn't make you stupid. It doesn't make you weak. It just makes you… human."

Her chin trembled.

"And?" she whispered.

"And if someone hurts you," I added, "that's on them. Not you."

She didn't argue. She just nodded, eyes filling.

"I don't know how to be around him," she admitted, voice small.

"Then don't," I said. "Not until you're ready."

"But what if he needs—"

"He needs a lot of things," I cut in, softer now. "But he doesn't get to need you at the expense of you."

I loved him. But she needed someone to say that aloud.

For both their sakes.

She closed her eyes. A tear slipped down her cheek. She didn't wipe it away.

I didn't reach for her hand. Not yet.

I let the silence sit and mean what it needed to.

I'm here. I see you. You don't have to carry this alone.

…*f*…

Rose

That afternoon in orchestra, I sat closer to Marilyn than I ever had before.

Not so close that we were touching. Just close enough that when the room felt too tight, I could feel her there — solid, calm, steady.

Gabriel walked in late.

His hair was messy. His shirt wrinkled. He looked like he had slept in his clothes.

Mrs. Dalton gave him a look but said nothing.

He took his seat in the cello section.

I could feel his eyes on me before I saw them. It was like warmth and cold all at once crawling up the back of my neck.

I didn't turn.

When we started playing, I focused so hard on the notes that my vision blurred around the edges. Count the beats. Watch the bowings. Breathe in two, out two. Do not think about his hands on the strings. Do not think about his hands in your hair. Do not think about—

My bow scratched across a note. Wrong. I flinched.

Beside me, Marilyn's tone stayed steady. "Breathe," she whispered again.

I did.

At one point, Mrs. Dalton had us restart a passage. As bows went up, I couldn't help it — my eyes flicked over to the cello section.

Gabriel was already looking at me.

Our gazes collided.

In that brief, awful second, I saw everything on his face:

Guilt. Fear. Shame. Love.

My chest clenched.

I looked away first.

I could not hold that much of him right then without breaking apart in front of everyone.

When rehearsal ended, I packed my things quickly.

I heard him say, "Rose—"

My whole body went rigid.

Marilyn stepped between us without making it look like she was stepping between us. She just moved forward slightly, her shoulder eclipsing him from my line of sight as we headed toward the door.

"We're going to be late to next period," she said lightly. "Come on."

I let her pull me along.

I heard his footsteps behind us stop.

I didn't turn back.

…ƒ…

Marilyn

94

It felt like standing in the middle of a bridge that had cracked straight down the center.

On one side, Gabriel. On the other, Rose.

Both hurting. Both confused. Both looking for something I couldn't give them at the same time.

Gabriel tried to catch my eye when class ended. I pretended not to notice. Not because I didn't care. Because I knew if I looked at him, I'd see the boy I grew up with begging me to fix something I couldn't.

Later, in the hallway, he finally caught up to me while Rose ducked into the bathroom.

"Mar," he said, voice frayed.

I stared at the lockers over his shoulder.

"Don't call me that right now," I said quietly.

He winced. "I… I don't know what to do."

"About what?" I asked. I knew. I needed him to say it.

"About her." His eyes flicked toward the girls' bathroom door.

"You give her space," I said. "You don't push. You don't pretend nothing happened."

His throat bobbed. "I didn't mean—"

"I know you didn't," I cut in, more harshly than I intended. I softened my tone. "But you did. And she is allowed to feel however she feels."

Tears burned at the corners of his eyes. "Do you hate me?"

I sighed, the sound heavy in my chest.

"No," I said. "I don't hate you. But I'm mad. And I'm hurt. And I'm not on your side right now. I'm on hers."

He nodded slowly, like each word added another weight to his shoulders. "I deserve that."

"You deserve help," I corrected quietly. "But I'm not the one who can give it to you this time."

He looked at the floor.

"And you deserve," I added, "to deal with what you did without making her hold your guilt for you."

He flinched. I think that landed.

The bathroom door opened behind me. Rose stepped out, eyes still red around the edges but dry now.

I turned my body slightly, shielding her by instinct.

"Ready?" I asked her.

She nodded.

Gabriel didn't say a word.

As we walked away, I felt him watching us go — the boy who used to walk with me down these halls, now standing still, alone.

It hurt. But some things needed to hurt so they could heal right.

…f…

Rose

That night, I lay in bed staring at the ceiling, replaying little moments in my mind.

Not just the bad ones.

The good ones.

The first time he made my nephews laugh. The way he'd looked at me when we practiced duets. The way he'd told me he loved me like it scared him. The way he asked, "Are you okay?"

after our first time and meant it.

And woven into all those memories was the sound of that quiet, awful silence in the next room. The weight of what he had chosen. The way he had not stopped it. The way he had said, "I'm a freak too," and how I had tried to help him hold that without breaking apart.

I didn't know what to do with all of that.

I only knew this:

I could not carry it alone.

And thanks to Marilyn — thanks to the way she sat beside me without demanding explanations, thanks to the way she nudged me away when I couldn't say "no" myself, thanks to the way she believed me without knowing the story —

I didn't have to.

We had never said the words "I promise" or "I'll protect you." We hadn't given our bond a name.

But in the spaces between words, in the glances across orchestra stands, in the quiet lunches by the lockers, something had been decided.

She would stand with me. I would lean on her.

And whatever happened with Gabriel next, we would not face the fallout alone.

That was the treaty.

Silent. Unwritten. Binding.

Forged in the space between two girls who loved different parts of the same boy and refused to let that be the thing that broke them.

CHAPTER 14
ROSE

One Last Good Day

There are days after a wound when the body still tries to pretend it is not hurt. I think the heart does the same.

A week after the night at Gabriel's house — after the dice, after Clay, after the silence between us grew into something that stood in every room we entered — I woke up and realized I missed him.

Not the version from that night. Not the version who wouldn't look at me after. Not the version who seemed terrified of his own shadow.

I missed *him.* The boy who played Bach with his whole soul. The boy who laughed with his shoulders. The boy who kissed me like he was grateful to have a mouth at all.

And for one morning, that ache outweighed the fear.

So when he texted —

Can we talk after school? — I typed *okay* before I could talk myself out of it.

…ƒ…

He waited outside the orchestra room, hands shoved deep into his hoodie pocket, shoulders hunched like he was bracing for the weather even though the hall was warm.

When he saw me, he straightened too quickly. Nervous. Hopeful. Fragile.

"Hey," he said.

It was such a small word, but it hit me like a memory.

"Hey." My voice sounded steadier than I felt.

For a second neither of us moved. Students walked around us, laughing, slamming lockers, living lives that weren't ours.

"You wanna go somewhere quiet?" he asked.

I nodded, and we took the long hallway toward the practice rooms — the one nobody used after hours because the acoustics were weird and one of the fluorescent lights buzzed so loudly it sounded like a swarm of insects.

It was perfect.

Inside the room, he leaned against the wall, arms folded. Not defensive — just unsure.

"I'm sorry," he said softly.

For a moment I didn't breathe.

"I know," I whispered. And I meant it. Even if the apology couldn't fix anything, I knew it cost him something to say it.

He looked at the floor, then at me, then away again. His eyes were tired — the kind of tired you don't get from staying up too late, but from carrying something too heavy for too long.

100

"I miss you," he said.

My chest tightened. "I miss you too."

That was the truth. A simple, hurting truth.

He exhaled shakily, like he hadn't expected me to say it back.

"Do you want to… play?" he asked, nodding toward the two cellos resting in the corner. "Just…" He shrugged. "Like we used to."

Something in him — and in me — needed this. A reminder that not every moment between us was broken.

"Yeah," I said. "Okay."

We tuned quietly. He plucked the A string twice; I matched him. For a moment it felt like time folded around us, like we were stepping back into the version of ourselves that hadn't unraveled yet.

We chose the first Bach suite. Of course we did. It lived in our bones.

He played the prelude first — slow at the beginning, then warmer. Not perfect. But honest. And when he reached the descending run, the one he always played too fast, he slowed down. Did it right.

For me.

When it was my turn, I felt something loosen inside my chest. Not forgiveness. Not forgetting. Just… breath.

We played through the allemande together, our bows rising and falling in quiet rhythm. There was no fire in it — just closeness. A soft, trembling thread trying to hold.

When we finished, he rested his bow across his knee,

staring at the floor.

"That felt… good," he said.

"It did," I agreed.

He looked up then — really looked at me — and the weight of it almost buckled my knees. There was so much in his expression: gratitude, fear, longing, shame, love. A whole storm he didn't know how to name, swirling behind his green eyes.

"I'm trying," he whispered.

"I know." I did. That was the hardest part.

He stepped closer, hesitated, then touched my wrist gently, like he was checking if I was still real.

For the first time since the Breaking, I didn't pull away.

His shoulders sagged with relief. He let out a small laugh — breathy, almost embarrassed. And for one fragile moment, the room felt warm again.

Not healed. Not whole. But warm.

We walked out together. He carried my cello case like he used to. I let him.

Outside, the evening air was soft and golden. The kind of weather that tricks you into believing things might be okay again.

He walked me to my mom's car. We stood there awkwardly.

"Can we… try?" he asked quietly.

I swallowed, heart twisting. "I don't know yet," I said. "But today was good."

His smile — small, tired, hopeful — was enough to make something in me break and mend at the same time.

"I'll take good," he said.

He leaned in, just enough to brush his forehead to mine. Not a kiss. Just closeness.

I let him.

Then the moment passed. My mom pulled up. I stepped back.

"See you tomorrow?"

"Maybe," I said.

The word tasted careful. Not a promise. Not a no.

He nodded, accepting it like a gift.

And for one last day, we were almost us again.

Almost.

But almost is a fragile thing.

It doesn't hold.

Not for long.

CHAPTER 15
MARILYN

The Boy She Remembers

There's a specific kind of grief that doesn't wait for someone to disappear. It hits while they're still close enough to touch, still living in your orbit, still breathing the same air — and yet so far away you can't recognize the shape of them anymore.

That was how it felt losing Gabriel.

He didn't die. He didn't move away. He didn't stop existing.

He just… faded.

Piece by piece.

Into someone I didn't know how to reach.

…*f*…

Rose was curling inward. I could see it in everything she did.

She didn't smile the same. Didn't talk the same. Didn't

laugh at the things she used to.

She leaned into me more — literally leaned, as if her body needed a place to rest that wasn't him. I let her. I held her in small ways, the ways that say *I see you* without demanding she explain herself.

I wanted to fix her. But I knew I couldn't.

And I wanted to be angry at Gabriel. But I couldn't do that cleanly, either.

Because I knew him. Not the version people whispered about in the hallways. Not the one who made bad choices. The boy who grew up beside me. The one who helped me catch fireflies in my backyard when we were nine. The one who used to call me "kid" even though we were the same age.

The one who used to be safe.

The one who wasn't anymore.

…ƒ…

The day of the phone call, Rose sat on the floor of my bedroom, knees pulled to her chest, eyes swollen but dry. Her breathing was thin and shaky — the kind you only hear when someone is deliberately holding themselves together.

She showed me the message Gabriel sent:

Can we talk? Please.

She didn't want to. She also didn't want *not* to.

That's how trauma works — it makes contradiction feel like truth.

She held the phone in trembling hands. I stayed beside her silently, letting her decide.

Finally, she hit call. She put it on speaker. I didn't ask her to — she just did.

Maybe she needed me there. Maybe she needed a witness.

Gabriel's voice came in breathless, too fast:

"Rose—please—I'm sorry, I'm so sorry, I never meant—"

She cut in, voice hard but breaking underneath: "Stop. Gabriel, stop."

Silence.

Then: "You twisted everything," she said, tears in her eyes. "You made it about you."

His voice cracked. "No—no, I didn't—Rose, I love you, I swear—"

"You hurt me!" she shouted suddenly. "You hurt me and you don't even understand how."

My chest tightened. He had no idea. He really didn't.

I jumped in — not to take over, but to anchor her:

"Rose is telling you how she feels," I said. "You need to listen."

He breathed sharply. "Marilyn… please don't—"

But I wasn't doing anything. I was standing with her. That was all.

He started spiraling — talking too fast, stumbling, apologizing and explaining and begging all at once.

Rose covered her mouth as tears spilled over.

"Gabriel," I said firmly. "You're not listening to her. You're drowning her out."

"I'm trying!" he insisted. "I'm trying so hard—"

"But you're hurting her," I said softly. "And you don't see it."

A long pause.

Then Rose whispered the sentence that broke all of us:

"You broke me, Gabriel. And you don't get to pretend you didn't."

The line went silent.

Then — click.

Call ended.

Rose collapsed into me, sobbing quietly. And I held her. And I didn't say anything. There was nothing left to say.

…ƒ…

I thought that would be the worst of it. It wasn't.

A week later, Gabriel showed up at my house.

I heard the knock first. My stomach dropped — I recognized it immediately. Three taps. Pause. One.

The knock he always used when we were kids.

"Mar?" he called through the door. His voice cracked. "Please—can I talk to you? Just for a minute?"

I froze in the hallway.

Part of me wanted to open the door. To let him in. To tell him I still loved him like a brother.

But my dad got there first.

He opened the front door only a few inches — just enough to see who it was.

Gabriel stood there — hair messy, eyes red, clutching the sleeves of his hoodie like a kid caught in the rain.

My dad's face hardened.

"Son," he said sternly, "you need to leave."

Gabriel blinked. "Mr. Hale—please—I just—"

108

"No." My dad's voice didn't rise. It didn't need to. "You are not welcome here anymore."

I saw Gabriel flinch through the crack in the door.

"I didn't mean—" he whispered.

"I don't care what you meant," Dad said. "You are hurting my daughter. You need to go."

Gabriel swallowed hard, jaw shaking. He nodded once — a small, broken motion — and stepped back.

He didn't run. He didn't argue. He didn't defend himself.

He just whispered, "I'm sorry," to the ground.

And my dad shut the door.

I stood frozen at the corner of the hallway, hand over my mouth.

Gabriel walked away slowly down the driveway, shoulders hunched, like the weight of his whole life had just been dropped on him at once.

And something inside me cracked open.

Not out of anger. Not out of righteousness. Out of grief.

The boy who grew up beside me had become someone my father — *my father,* who had loved him like a son — no longer recognized as safe.

And the worst part?

I didn't disagree.

…ƒ…

That night, I sat on my bed staring at the wall, thinking about fireflies and cello lessons and the first time he called me "family."

I thought about Rose's sobs. About the way he said her

109

name on the phone. About the way she leaned into me afterward, trembling.

I thought about my dad's voice — steady, protective, final.

And I thought about Gabriel standing on our porch, looking like he would fall apart if someone breathed on him wrong.

I loved him. I loved the boy he was. The boy he tried to be. The boy trauma didn't give him permission to become.

But I couldn't follow him into the dark.

Not when Rose needed me. Not when he didn't know how to stop hurting the people who loved him. Not when every step closer to him felt like stepping into a collapsing building.

So I let him go.

Not because I wanted to. Because staying would have broken all three of us.

That's the thing about childhood friends: you don't always get to keep them.

Sometimes the world takes them from you piece by piece, until all you can do is hold the memory of who they were and pray the world gives them a softer landing than it gave you.

Gabriel wasn't mine to save anymore. He hadn't been for a long time.

And letting him go hurt more than anything he ever did.

But I did it anyway.

Because sometimes love means stepping away before the fire spreads.

CHAPTER 16
ROSE

The Last Thread Snaps

There comes a point in grief where the heart gives up on announcing the pain. It just goes quiet.

That's what happened with Gabriel and me.

There was no breakup speech, no screaming match in a hallway, no dramatic exit that people whispered about for weeks. It was smaller than that. Quieter.

It was the slow unthreading of something that had already torn.

…ƒ…

The week after the phone call, everything between us felt suspended in a kind of slow, cold drifting. Not hateful. Not angry.

Just… fading.

He sat further away in orchestra. Not intentionally — I

don't think he could have orchestrated anything that carefully anymore — but because he didn't know where to put himself.

He kept his head down. Barely spoke. Barely breathed.

And I didn't know how to be near him without shaking.

It wasn't fear of him. It was fear of myself — fear of what the closeness would demand, fear of the memories that wouldn't stay quiet, fear of how much I still cared.

Every time he tried to catch my eye, something inside me twisted.

But I couldn't hold his gaze. Not without breaking.

So I looked at the music. At the strings. At anything else.

My "maybe" became my shield.

"Maybe we can talk." "Maybe we can hang out later." "Maybe next week."

But "maybe" was just a softer way to say "no," and we both knew it.

...f...

There was one moment — one fragile, blinking moment — where it felt like we might repair something.

It was after rehearsal. I stayed behind to put my music away, hands shaking just enough to slow me down.

He lingered too. I could feel him gathering courage like someone preparing to step into a storm.

"Rose?" he whispered.

My heart clenched. I didn't turn around right away. I didn't trust my face.

When I did, he looked smaller than I remembered. Not in size — in presence. Like he was made of paper now instead of bone.

112

His eyes were soft, scared, pleading in a way that almost undid me.

"I'm sorry," he said.

Not the frantic babbling from the call. Not the panicked desperation.

Just one sentence, quiet and trembling.

And I realized something in that moment — something I had been avoiding for weeks:

I still loved him. Even after everything. Even when I shouldn't.

But love didn't erase what happened. It didn't rebuild trust. It didn't quiet the fear or the confusion or the ache.

It just sat there, beating quietly under the hurt.

"I know," I said. And I meant it.

But that wasn't enough to pull us back together.

We stood there in the dim light of the practice room, staring at each other across a few feet that felt like miles. He waited for something — forgiveness, maybe. A new beginning. A final chance.

I didn't have it in me.

So I offered the only truth I could:

"I don't think we can keep doing this."

He swallowed, eyes dropping to the floor. His shoulders folded inward, like he was trying to make himself smaller.

"I know," he said. Barely audible.

There were a thousand things I wanted to tell him — that he wasn't evil, that he wasn't broken beyond repair, that I wished things had been different, that I hoped one day he would understand he wasn't a monster.

But none of those words made it to the surface.

All I could manage was:

"Goodnight, Gabriel."

He flinched at the formality. Like my using his full name was worse than any goodbye.

"Goodnight," he whispered back.

I walked away first.

And this time, he didn't follow.

…f…

The next day, I found out he wasn't allowed at Marilyn's house anymore. Her dad told him he wasn't welcome. I didn't blame him.

But something inside me cracked at the thought of Gabriel standing on that porch, being turned away by the man who once treated him like a son.

I sat in my room that night, staring at the wall, thinking about everything we had been — the laughter, the duets, the whispered secrets on the phone, the way he looked at me like I was something worth choosing.

I thought about the good parts of him. The parts no one else saw. The parts he tried so hard to protect. The parts the world crushed out of him long before I ever knew him.

And I realized:

We didn't lose each other in a single moment. We lost each other in pieces.

A thousand tiny fractures. A thousand quiet hurts. A thousand chances to speak that we never took.

He was the boy I loved. He was the boy I couldn't save. He

114

was the boy who needed someone stronger than I could be.

And letting him go didn't feel like giving up. It felt like mercy.

For him. For me.

For the versions of us that never got the chance to grow the way they deserved.

…*f*…

Years from now, people will talk about high school love like it's something small, something forgettable.

But I will remember.

I will remember the music and the laughter and the soft way he held his bow. I will remember the warmth of his forehead pressed to mine. I will remember the way he said my name like it mattered.

And I will remember the heartbreak — quiet, slow, inevitable — that taught me what it meant to love someone without being able to keep them.

This was our ending. Not perfect. Not clean.

But real.

And I will carry the good parts of him the way you carry a bruise — tender, permanent, and never without feeling something.

THE END

Acknowledgments

Thank you to Marilyn and Rose — the two who loved Gabriel in ways he never fully understood. You carried him, challenged him, and finally let him go. This book is proof that side characters aren't side characters at all. You matter. Your stories matter. Your pain matters.

To the readers who followed OWAB and came here hungry for more: thank you. You carried these characters with you long after the last page, and that means more than I can say.

To those who have loved someone who was breaking — to those who tried to help, to those who had to walk away, to those who still feel the echo of it: you're seen.

To every friend, mentor, and believer who pushed me to keep writing, thank you for reminding me that stories deserve to breathe even when life feels heavy.

And to the survivors, the quiet fighters, the ones living with memories you didn't ask for — your strength shaped every line of this novella.

Thank you for trusting me with your time, your heart, and your hope.

Author's Note

This book exists because stories rarely happen to one person alone.

In *Of Wolves & Butterflies*, Gabriel's trauma ripples outward — into childhood friendships, first love, and the fragile bonds of trust that form around him. While his voice carried the novel, the impact of his pain fell heavily on others.

This novella is for the "others."

For the friend who watched him change and didn't know why. For the girl who loved him deeply and paid a price for it. For the people who held their breath while he broke. For the ones he hurt without meaning to.

These pages honor their experiences — the confusion, the fear, the loyalty, the heartbreak, and the complicated tenderness that comes with loving someone who is hurting.

If you have ever loved someone through their darkest seasons… If you have ever walked away because staying would have broken you… If you have ever carried someone else's story in your chest… I hope you feel seen here.

Thank you for giving Marilyn and Rose their own voices.

— **Brandon Thomason**

Other Works by Brandon Thomason
Of Wolves & Butterflies

COMING SOON

***Black Gold, Red Hands* Anthology**

Each story stands alone — but the oilfield connects them all.

Book One – *Black Gold, Red Hands* – Spring 2026

A roughneck trying to outrun his past becomes entangled in new

oilfield deaths that echo his past tragedy.

Themes: Guilt, manipulation, trauma.

Book Two – *The Saltwater Line* – Fall 2026

A truck driver's son vanishes amid human trafficking masked as

oil transport.

Themes: Love, vengeance, the cost of protection.

Book Three – *The Hollow Derrick* – Spring 2027

An environmental scientist unravels a contamination cover-up tied

to the same corporation.

Themes: Truth, obsession, moral decay.

Book Four – *Ash on the Wind* – Fall 2027

A journalist investigates ritualized suicides among oil workers and

uncovers a cult-like network of executives.

Themes: Faith, superstition, the price of truth.

Book Five – *Blood Beneath the Pumpjack* – Summer 2028

Eli Ward returns to uncover the truth about his brother's death and

confront the cost of redemption.

Themes: Redemption, legacy, atonement.

About the Author

Brandon Thomason is a storyteller who has lived enough life to know that pain shapes us, love saves us, and hope is rarely loud. He writes from experience, from scars, and from the parts of himself most people never see.

A husband, father of four, actor, musician, ministry student, and lifelong observer of people, Brandon channels every corner of his world into his work. His writing pulls from childhood wounds, faith reconstruction, unexpected friendships, and the beauty found in flawed, complicated characters.

He wrote *Of Wolves & Butterflies* as a raw reflection of shame, survival, and the fight to reclaim identity. He wrote *Loving Him In Pieces* because side characters are never really side characters — they carry the story too.

Brandon lives in Texas, balancing family, work, church, theatre, and writing with the kind of exhaustion that only comes from loving deeply and giving fully. He writes for the quiet ones, the hurting ones, the ones still trying to figure out who they are in the aftermath of everything they survived.

He hopes his stories remind readers they are not alone.

You can connect with Brandon online:

Website: www.BrandonThomasonAuthor.com

Instagram: @Brandon_D_Thomason_Author

TikTok: @booktokwithb7

Facebook: https://www.facebook.com/BDTNovelist

Some stories don't end with a goodbye.

Some end with healing that begins in silence.